SCH (G)

WITHDRAWN

CATCH AND OTHER STORIES

Catch
and Other Stories

by

Stephen Bowkett

LONDON
VICTOR GOLLANCZ LTD
1988

First published in Great Britain 1988
by Victor Gollancz Ltd,
14 Henrietta Street, London WC2E 8QJ

British Library Cataloguing in Publication Data
Bowkett, Stephen
  Catch and other stories.
  I. Title
  823′.914[F]

ISBN 0-575-04399-7

Photoset and printed in Great Britain
by WBC Print Ltd, Bristol.

To Des and Stella,
With Deepest Affection

Contents

She Bites

Her eyes said come and get me, and all of us lads in the third year would do anything for her. Eleanor Garou had moved to the area a year ago and had been the centre of attention ever since, though nobody *I* ever talked to knew much about her. What I knew was what I could see, and I suppose that was enough. . .

She was tall—probably an inch over my five-feet-eight—and dark: her hair was long and straight, with a deep blue-blackness that shone, yet seemed not to reflect any light: her eyebrows were sharp streaks, slanted a little to give her a catlike look: her chin was pointed rather than rounded, her smile white and gleaming and always ambiguous. And her eyes. . . I always thought that she was looking at the world from behind them, instead of through them, as though they hid big secrets—like two-way mirrors.

All of this had led me, and the rest of the football first eleven, to fall in love with her. It was not only the way she looked of course—though the leotard she wore to gym sessions had a lot to do with it—no, it was also the air of mystery she carried with her, and the fact that no-one had succeeded in taking her out all year, which allowed the rest of us to live in hope.

She was clever, too: never seemed to struggle for 'A's in termtime assignments, and she cruised through with top marks in all subjects when the exams arrived. Strange thing, none of the other girls grew jealous. Perhaps she flew the banner of the female cause too well for that, or maybe they knew that they'd just make fools of themselves if they tried to beat her.

In fact, the only kid in existence who must have disapproved of Eleanor Garou was a little squirt in the second year called David Nimbley; class boff and also my cousin. I guess that was the sole reason I ever listened to him, and possibly because he was also, in his own quirky way, as clever as she was. The difference between them was that Ellie had a wonderful textbook knowledge, whereas Dave knew all kinds of odd things: trivia, fragments, miscellanies of useless facts. He understood about leylines and earth-magic, alchemy, Vlad the Impaler, quasars, pulsars and black holes: he could tell you how to survive in the Sahara using only what you carried in your pockets, or when eels migrate to the Sargasso Sea to mate: he knew how to blend the juices from garden plants to cure a headache or ease arthritis, or where King Arthur was supposed to be buried. . . All pretty pointless, of course, if you wanted to become an accountant or a computer programmer.

We were sort of friends and had been since early junior school. I kept David from being bullied—lots of kids were tempted to push their fists into his pale bucktoothed face—and he told me how to protect myself against Wendigoes and divine for water if I was ever thirsty on a hillwalk. It was Dave who let me in on the fact that Eleanor was a vampire.

I'd stopped late one night for ski-training. The P.E. staff arranged an annual trip to Austria in February, and I'd always had a hankering to go skiing. I'd missed out so far (broken ankle in the first year, lack of money in the second), and was determined to make it before I moved from the High School to the Upper School and got entangled in careers options, exam courses and the like. Exercise sessions began

8

soon after the autumn term started—in mid October—and became progressively more demanding until we were all so fit that skiing for six hours a day would be a pushover.

Anyway, I came away from school at six o'clock feeling pretty tired. All I wanted to do was get home, have some tea and then collapse in front of the TV. When I saw Dave lingering around the main gate, I didn't know whether to run the other way, ignore him completely as I walked past, or ask him what was wrong. I sighed and bit back my impatience.

"Hi Dave. What's wrong?"

He scurried across, sort of shrewlike, and put his arm through my arm as a young brother might do. His grey eyes were ferrety and nervous.

"Listen, Colin," he said, "you're in trouble. Big trouble, you understand?"

"Trouble eh. If it's about the maths homework I copied off Specky Rowlands. . . Don't tell me he got *every* answer wrong!"

"Nothing like that." David glanced around himself, left-right-upwards. We scuttled across the road into the southern estate, making for home.

"It's about that girl, Eleanor Garou, in Miss Roberts's class."

"Now I'm listening."

"She's a vampire."

He said it in the same tone he'd use to tell me that her starsign was Capricorn, or that she wore size seven trainers. I nodded, quenching my smile.

"Right. I must stock up on garlic then and get hold of a stake. Actually, steak's lovely with garlic."

"I'm being serious, Colin!"

"Yeah, and so am I—now push off and go and turn lead into gold or something. . . Anyway, how do you know?"

Dave stopped walking; stopped *me* walking and looked me straight in the eyes. Under the orange streetlight, his face was like a mask, one of those Greek Tragedy masks you sometimes see in drama books.

"Threads of evidence, woven together. . ."

"Dave, I'm warnin' ya."

"Her eyebrows meet in the middle. She never looks in the mirror. She stays indoors on sunny days."

"That's about *it*—"

"And I've seen her in St Mary's graveyard."

A light prickle of shock ran electrically along my neck.

"Short cut home," I snapped back. Dave shook his head slowly, confidently.

"She *has* no home, Col. The address in the register says 'Plot Six, Lilith Way'. Well there is no Lilith Way, not yet leastways. It's on the development plans in the town library, but at the moment it's just open waste ground next to the church. Plot Six abuts the cemetery—as close as you can get without being on sanctified soil."

"Is that all?" I asked, a little hollowly. Dave chuckled with nerves.

"Well. . . I've watched her, followed her. She *always* uses the path across the graveyard. And—and she stares at the moon!"

"So do you."

"I'm an astronomer," Dave threw back, offended. "She just—stares. And last time, two nights ago, she reached up for it and moaned. Honest, Col, I nearly wet myself!"

Now my smile was wide and easy. Dave's face was sinking into the dusk, but I could see that he was still worried.

"She's got you really wound up tight, mate. Don't you realise that Eleanor must've guessed you were following her, and put that on just for show—simply to scare you?"

I flapped my hand at him and turned away. Turned back.

"Besides, why are you letting *me* in on this? I mean, I know I'm desperately in love with—"

"Because she's after you, Colin," Dave said, the words bitten off with resentment and hurt. "Rumours are already going round. She's *after* you, understand?"

I grinned. "That's all right by me. I might condescend to let her take me out, after a little chasing you understand. . ."

"Yeah, well. . ." Dave shrugged. His streetlight-orange face looked lost. "I've warned you and that's all I can do."

"Thanks Dave. I appreciate your concern. See you around."

"OK," he said, and then, out of the darkness as he walked away: "Just be careful, Colin. She bites."

"Hi. I'm Colin Williams."

I put my dinner plate down and sat opposite her, tingling with anticipation, nervous because of the way I'd dared myself. People from other tables were glancing across: I saw Specky Rowlands nudge his mate's elbow.

Eleanor looked up and smiled: I'm here, what are you going to do about it? she said without speaking. I started to tangle myself up in alternative plans. . .

"Um. Look, do you mind if I sit here?"

"No, not at all." Her voice was velvety smooth. She brushed back her hair and returned to her meal.

"You like salad?" I nearly laughed with relief to watch her knifing coleslaw and lettuce on to her fork.

"Mmmm. Keeps the hunger pangs away."

"Listen, em, Ellie, I—"

I could hardly believe how I sounded: like a total amateur, bumbling my way in nailed boots while Eleanor's calm sophistication remained unchallenged. And I nearly cried as my voice stumbled to a halt and hot embarrassment crept over my face.

"I'm free on Friday," she said quietly, with beautiful gentleness, and lifted her eyes to me. They were dark and glittering, gorgeous, impenetrable, reflecting my questions.

"Well, yes, I was going to ask. . ."

The opportunity was there and I leaped at it.

"How about if I meet you at seven? We could go to the cinema, or there's a play on at the theatre. . ."

"I'm not into *amateur* dramatics," Ellie said. "A walk maybe. Get to know each other."

That sounded even better. "Right. You live out to the west of town don't you?" She nodded. "I'll meet you by the church, then, at seven."

"Sharp," Eleanor said. Sunlight was coming in through the big panoramic windows along one side of the dining hall, and she didn't flinch once.

I found Lilith Way on the drawings in the library, and on Friday after school I checked it out 'in the field'. It was in the field too, or thereabouts: only a stretch of chewed-up ground that the diggers had been over in the summer, tufted with autumn-withered grass and littered with flints and broken half-bricks dredged up from long buried cottages. No-one had lived there for years (I hoped).

Just nearby was the graveyard, as Dave had said, and beyond that St Mary's church in its grounds. Facing that way, north and east, the sky was gloomy; dark bulked shapes of yew trees rising against built-up clouds that were another shade of deep grey. Westward the sun was near to setting, all spilled out red and gold along the skyline.

I waited, and thought about things. The lights of the town sparkled half a mile away, linking themselves to me by a single sparse row of lamps that defined the direction of the church road. It was empty of traffic. I began to feel lonely.

What if Eleanor had been winding *me* up, as well? I wondered. Maybe she wanted to teach me a lesson, get me shivering-scared out here so that I'd scuttle back to school and start adding to Dave's vampire theory. Perhaps that was her kind of humour, sort of cold and distant, preying on people's gullibility. Could be she was standing right close to me at this moment, watching me getting edgy, frightened, terrified. . .

I turned around, trying to be casual, as a breeze lifted the arms of the yew trees and hissed in the laurel bushes that lined the gravel church-paths.

Out of the shadows came a shadow.

"Ellie!"

"Sorry I'm late, Colin. I had some homework."

To my huge pleasure and relief Eleanor whispered this close in my ear, and let her lips touch my cheek before she drew away. Her hand traced a path down my arm and found my hand, and held it. My pride began to glow.

"I was getting worried."

"Sorry," she said again, facing me. She was night-cool and smelt of a strange perfume that slipped away the second I tried to identify it. She wore, from what I could see of her in the twilight, a heavy pale jumper, jeans, dark shoes that might have been trainers: casual and practical, but they still flattered her.

"You'll get cold," I said. Eleanor gave a soft, deep laugh, like a sigh.

"I don't think so."

"Let's walk, then: keep the circulation going."

I was glad to leave Lilith Way behind. It was a name and an idea with no reality behind it.

"Where to?"

I was hoping for town, and began gently to steer her that way, but her hand answered by tugging, away from the road to the church.

We passed beneath the lych gate and along the packed

13

gravels of the path, that made a rich crunching sound under our shoes. The sky was almost completely dark now, all piled up masses of black cloud with a few gaps between, through which the royal blue of the evening showed: in one gap glimmered a single star.

Beside me Eleanor was silent. I could not even hear her breathing. We walked up to the looming hulk of the church and stepped under its porch. Then she spoke so suddenly that my brittle control shattered and my body tensed.

"See there?" She pointed to a triangular space between the lintel and the arch, a cut out shape of black. "It's a tympanum, put there to represent St Dunstan's fight with the Devil. There's a rhyme about it:

> 'St Dunstan, as the story goes,
>   Caught Old Sathanus by the nose:
> He tugged so hard and made him roar
>   That he was heard three miles and more.' "

She giggled lightly. "Can you *imagine* that sound!"

"No," I muttered, and wouldn't want to, I added to myself.

Ellie unlatched the heavy wooden door, pushed it aside and took me in. The church was a place of motionless cold. I smelt old stones, stale candlewax and the faint fustiness of the carpets that lay along the aisles. The walls breathed out echoes.

"Spooky," I said, hushed, and the air sizzled with my sound.

"It shouldn't be. A church is a holy place, a safe place, eh Colin? This one is Norman. It's supposed to be built on the site of an older church, Anglo-Saxon, that was made of wood and thatch. Stave-kirks they were called: long decayed away. . ."

14

I was struck by a powerful sense of the absurd. Here I stood, alone with the girl I'd wanted to date all year, a hot-blooded male all ready to prove myself. . . And we were talking about early Christian antiquities. I laughed, disliked the boom of noise, and shut up.

"Why are we here, Eleanor?" I asked seriously. I had arrived because of a chance, a dare and a fantasy: but now it was real and my body was cold and what Dave had said weighed heavily in my mind.

Ellie faced me and moved close. The perfume of her again. Her cool breath near my mouth. Her body against me.

"Because I know," she said, "that you wanted proof from me."

"Proof?"

"That what your cousin said wasn't true. How can it be, when I'm standing here under the eye of the cross, not in agony, not withering to dead leaves in front of you. Do *you* think I'm some kind of freak, Colin?"

I felt ashamed and brushed aside my alarm that Eleanor knew of my conversation with Dave. I put my hand to her head and urged her closer. Her hair was shadows. I kissed her and it was sweet and normal. I could see her. I could see her now!

"The moon," she said, and took my hand and walked with me along the nave towards the eastward facing window of stained glass. "It's beautiful."

Suddenly I was still not sure. Would she melt into a thing of wings and fangs at my side, glare with red eyes and that demon's grin I'd seen on a hundred late-night movies?

No. She stayed the same, smiling as we both watched saints and angels glow like rainbows in patterns of coloured glass.

"I'm sorry, Ellie," I began, "I really am, about this—"

"Ahh," she groaned, "the beautiful moon."

I wasn't scared at all: just held still, as though nailed there, to feel the hairs that were crawling out of the skin of her palm.

Gurney

I want to write this down now, just after it's happened, because in six months I don't think I'll believe it myself: no-one will believe it anyway. . .

When you start at a new school, there are ways of making the transition easy on yourself. I know this because when my family moved up to the Midlands and I joined the first year at Beckford Comprehensive I thought hard about the problem and decided that the best way to avoid trouble was to sort of slide invisibly into the new routines. Making waves, trying too hard to be accepted or popular, only brings you to the attention of teachers just itching to make you feel awkward and foolish. And it attracts the bullies, the kind who like to have a crack against any new kid, simply to prove that they're tougher and stronger.

I survived, suffering only one minor encounter with Len Donovan out of the fourth year. He came up to me one day, pushed me over and put his foot down across my neck as I lay there.

"Feeling lucky today, wimp?" he asked.

"Len Donovan?" I croaked. "Naa, not after what I've heard about you. . ."

His sneer of arrogance and aggression moderated towards puzzlement, became a little lopsided.

"Listen, people tell me you're the king around here, and I can see why. You're tougher than I'll ever be. Come on, do you think I'm stupid or something? I've heard you're the big man around here. . ."

17

Someone nearby laughed at all this rubbish. I turned fiercely.

"You're disagreeing that Donovan's the best?"

The grin on a little blond boy's face snapped off.

I turned back to Donovan.

"Anyway, you could flatten me in ten seconds or less. I'm not even worth bothering with. . ."

I shrugged, and there rested my case. Donovan seemed to ponder this hard for a while, then stuck out his square lower jaw and jabbed a big finger in my direction.

"Yeah, well jus' don't get out of line, OK?"

"Yeah, you know me, right?"

He drifted away like a pike in a pondful of minnows, searching after more prey. Happily the kids who'd been watching all this didn't voice their suspicions. Even more happily, the incident caught the attention of Samantha Lewis who appreciated the brilliance of my ploy and did not see it as a complete coward's way out of trouble. My first encounter with *her* is something I don't intend to talk about here. . .

Sheer bluff is one method of staying out of trouble. There are others. But when Scott Gurney appeared at the school after autumn half term, he went out of his way to get noticed.

First off, there was his name, not designed to camouflage one safely within a class of Davids, Andrews, Simons and Peters. Secondly there was the fact that 'gurning' means making a funny face, something usually done by toothless old men at village fêtes, when they've had a few pints of stout at the local.

Maybe Scott knew this, or maybe not: however much of a coincidence it was, he actually made funny faces to attract attention!

And he was good at it. He was not the best looking kid in the world. . . Not even quite normal-looking in fact. He had pale, straight hair, not so much fair as just colourless, washy blue eyes that stared like a fish (one of Donovan's minnows, I couldn't help thinking), a big bulbous nose, thickish red lips and a large mole on his right cheek. The effect was strange rather than ugly, and it made him look unintelligent, though in fact his voice was crisp and articulate. He had brains, just didn't seem to know how to use them.

I remember the first time I saw him gurning. It was at break on about the third day back after the half term holidays. Scott was standing in the sun, looking bewildered or dreamy, and a few kids from his form were passing by. One of them yelled, "Hey Gurney, give us a face!"

And of course he did, and a crowd gathered.

I gathered too, mainly because I'd heard rumours of this trick he had. I was curious, and I felt sorry for him though I didn't yet know him.

"What do you want?" Scott asked, a smart voice coming out of a dull mouth.

"Make us laugh."

"He already does," someone shouted. Everyone guffawed. More came to watch the circus.

And he began. First he did what most kids can do, the pig-monster face—thumb and third finger pulling on the skin below the eyes, index finger pushing up at the nose. Not much response to that one.

Then Scott attempted a traditional gurning face, turning his eyes inward so that only the whites showed, sucking in his cheeks to make his mouth pucker like the blowhole of a balloon. How he did it with a mouthful of teeth I didn't know—not then.

A few kids were leaving the frayed edges of the crowd, but more were joining. We all had the feeling I think that more, and the best, was yet to come.

"Try a dog," came another request.

"Lovely with chips!"

People cheered and laughed. Scott smiled stupidly.

He tried the dog and the crowd fell silent. We all saw him do it, but no-one was able to say how: and when he stood before us and howled, a couple of kids moaned and one ran off—I hoped to fetch a teacher.

First he stuck his head forward so that his lump of a nose jutted out. Then he sort of rolled back his lips to show deep pink gums, opened his mouth wider so that white teeth glittered in the sun. His canines seemed long and prominent. Scott hunched his back, drew up his hands like paws. He grunted, gave a bark. His ears seemed to be pointed now, just like a dog's ears.

People started to mutter, impressed and a little unnerved. A group of first year girls giggled uneasily, sounding exactly like I felt. The noise began to swell and then someone clapped. Applause crackled through with the speed of a forest fire, kids cheered. One yelled,

"Now do Mr Meres! Go on!"

Any new people at Beckford found out about Meres in the first few hours. He was the deputy head, a short hunchbacked man who must once have been in the army: whiplash voice, perpetual scowl, hard unforgiving eyes. He hated kids and we hated him. But we feared him even more.

Scott chuckled, appreciating the challenge. His dog's face melted and he flowed easily into a beautiful mime of Meres. His back seemed to bubble up under his blazer into the exact shape of Meres' hump: he stopped, made his eyes freeze over, did something with his eyebrows so that they looked longer and darker. Scott's mouth tightened in. He said, "Now you brats, you will line up outside my office—AT ONCE!"

That was too realistic to be comfortable. The voice snapped and echoed back off the school buildings—not Scott's voice, but the dreaded sound of Mr Meres in one of his

Armageddon moods. It shut everybody up as effectively as if Meres himself had been standing there.

No applause came this time, only a slow realisation—spreading ever faster—that Meres *was* there, fetched out by the kid who'd run off.

A silence descended, one of those silences that seemed to be made of bone china. Nobody wanted to look at Meres for fear of catching his eye: a few furtive heads slid towards Scott.

Slowly he came back to himself, straightened up, the teacherish scowl dissolving. Clouds drifted back over his face and he was Scott Gurney once more, a dumbo in a dream.

But Meres had seen, and must have guessed what fun was being had at his expense—maliciously on everyone else's part, for other reasons as far as Scott was concerned.

"And WHAT do you think YOU'RE about?" Meres snapped, the words as sharp as pistol shots.

"Pardon?"

"Pardon SIR!"

"Pardon sir. . ."

Some kids were departing, doing their best to pretend that they had only been casually passing by anyway, and *certainly* had no intention of standing around to watch the rise being taken out of Mr Deputy Headmaster Meres Sir Your Highness. . . A hard core of the stupid and the curious remained, daring Meres' wrath upon themselves. I suppose I counted myself as a little of both, watching as Scott was verbally beaten up and dissected, then grabbed by the ear and hauled off to The Office wherein, it was rumoured—always in a funeral ceremony voice—hung the heads of Beckford pupils unwise enough to cross Mr Meres before his back was fully turned.

Maybe it was my imagination, but as Scott trotted beside Meres with his head cocked ridiculously to the side, the ear in the little man's fingers seemed to soften like warm plasticene:

soften and stretch so that Scott, if he'd wanted to, could have pulled free any time he'd liked. . .

As it happened, I got to know him just as news of his escapade was spreading around the school. He was put next to me in French, at the desk by the window with our backs to the class. My reason for being there was that my command of French amounted to one or two swear words I'd learned from the locals on a day trip to Boulogne, and an oily Ooo-la-la whenever Sam Lewis passed by. She was in the same group, but at the top.

I think that Miss Bethnick put Scott with me not from any compassionate motive to give me company, but because the boy scared her. She had probably heard about what went on in the playground, just like everyone else, and it worried her. It was true, too, that Scott was pretty weird to look at. Which is why she chose not to look at him, telling him instead to "get on quietly with something" until she had a chance to test his vocabulary.

So we found ourselves together. I waited until Miss Bethnick had finished giving out her instructions, and the class was humming busily, supposedly practising verbs. Then I nudged Scott gently to get his attention and said out of the corner of my mouth:

"Hiya. I'm Nicholas Green—"

"I'm Scott Gurney."

"I know. And keep your voice down. Do you want to land in trouble *again*?"

He chuckled at that, a low and somehow sinister sound that made me shiver, despite the fact that the double desk faced a radiator, and my feet were propped against hot pipes. I could see suddenly why he gave some teachers the creeps. . . Just something about him.

"What did Meres do to you?" I wondered a few minutes

later. Miss Bethnick had done the rounds and prodded us both in the back for our chattering and empty workbooks.

"Ruler across the hand," came the reply. I was shocked.

"He can't do that! Not in this day and age."

"Well he did," Scott said. "But it didn't hurt, not if you hold your hand slack, like this."

He showed me, making a shallow cup of his right hand so that the flesh was ruttled and cushioned, the heel of the thumb uppermost to take the flat edge of the ruler.

I nodded—stopped nodding—and began to see that something was not quite right with his skin. Like his hair, like his face, the skin of his hand was pale and almost see-through, and it wasn't red and inflamed as it should have been, either. But there was another thing, something elusive about it that I couldn't quite—

Then Scott pulled his hand back as Miss Bethnick descended on us again.

"Is this the thanks I get for allowing you two to sit next to each other, hm? Well, speak up!"

"Sorry, miss," I began weakly. "I was only trying to make him feel at home. . ."

"And you, Scott?" Miss Bethnick demanded sternly, her voice heavy with suspicion and disbelief.

Scott stared at her and smiled.

"Sorry, miss, he was only trying to make me feel at home," he said in Mr Meres' voice.

I nearly creased up.

I found myself hanging about with Scott after that without really intending to. It was the curiosity thing again. The crisp smoothness of his voice by itself told me that the kid wasn't stupid. . . It was like he was far ahead of us, not needing the ordinary kind of education that Beckford Comp could give him, but here anyway for reasons of his own.

23

Besides, I wanted to see more of his gurning.

I asked him about it one day after school. We went to Bevin's on the corner for sweets, then wandered slowly up the long straight length of East Street towards the top estate where I lived.

"Where'd you learn to, uh, make faces, Scott?" I asked him, right out.

"Always been able to do it," he said back, easily able to chew a mouthful of gum *and* speak perfectly clearly at the same time. His rubbery lips turned up. "It's the only reason people want to know me."

I began to protest. "Oh, come on. . ."

"Except, I think, for you Nick. You're the only one who calls me 'Scott'. Everyone else yells out 'Gurney'—or worse."

"Well," I said, "it's tough having no friends at a new school. I hated the first few weeks here."

"Yeah, but now you're accepted, part of the crowd. People will never get used to me. . ."

"You didn't exactly go to much trouble to blend in. . . And why'd you take the bait and mimic old Meres?"

Scott shrugged, a fluid rippling of shoulders. "I like to be liked. Who doesn't? And it's what I'm good at."

"Fancy the stage, eh? Being a star?"

"A star?"

"Never mind. Anyway. . ." I said it to stop the conversation rolling downhill. "If you're *so* good, impress me with something."

"What d'you like?"

"Miss Bethnick," I shot back at once, testing him right from the start because she was sort of bland, not easy to caricature like Meres, who might have stepped complete from a Dickens novel.

Scott smiled, lifted his eyebrows a little, pursed up his lips and wagged a finger under my nose.

24

"Is this the thanks I get for allowing you two to sit next to each other, hm? Well, speak up!"

It was perfect! I hooted with laughter and knew I'd never be able to look our French teacher in the face ever again.

"Blobber Jones now," I suggested: Scott's head seemed to grow until it was a red full-moon split by Blobber's silly ever-innocent grin.

"Dork," I said next—the idiot of the class.

"Gi's a sweet. . ." Dork's sandpapery voice came back at once.

"Me."

That scared me to say it, but all of Scott's impersonations were effortless, and I considered myself a difficult subject to copy.

This time, he turned away, bending his head so that I could see nothing of him. The afternoon had been cloudy, building towards rain. Now in the gloom the first speckling drops tickled my face and the backs of my hands: Scott's body was a greyer bulk a yard from me. I began to dread what he would show me, but I had to see it too. I had to.

Then he straightened, turning back, smiling, my face on his shoulders.

"Where'd you, uh, learn to make faces, Scott?" Scott said, my voice in his mouth.

Maybe in the sunlight I could have seen faults, seen how he'd done it. This was more than a lifting of the eyebrows, a hunching of the back, something I'd never come across before. It was—not—normal.

I think Scott expected praise, or pride maybe. I guess he wanted me to be impressed. And I was, so impressed that I was terrified.

I stood the look in my own eyes for no more than three seconds, then spun round and ran full belt back towards school. A car coming down East Street with its headlights

25

already on blared its horn at me. I took no notice. I just ran.

Behind me, and over the swish of the car passing, came the voice:

"See you Nick. See you tomorrow. . ."

Words that belonged to nobody at all.

I did the stupid thing, of course, and followed him home the next night. Still, I suppose I was only coming up to the expectations of half the adults who knew me.

I explained to Scott in the morning, in a blustering and evasive way, that in the dim light the night before I could have sworn I was staring into a mirror, and that it had scared me.

"Try it now and I bet I pick you up on all the faults. . ."

Scott didn't try it, nor did he attempt any more gurning or mimicking that day.

He told me he lived out of town towards Draybrooke. I checked in his form's register and found his address as Manor Farm, Draybrooke—a place that I knew had been empty and shut down for years.

I deliberately lost myself from him in the corridor push at the end of lessons, but kept him in sight and tailed him at a good distance, past the War Memorial and the golf course and out along the Draybrooke Road.

After a mile he turned off towards Manor Farm, but walked by the padlocked entrance gate and on to a lay-by. Parked there was a big touring caravan—one of those 'fifties-looking ones with plenty of chrome trim, like gypsy vans—and a big Ford truck.

Someone was standing in the open doorway of the caravan, looking back the way we'd come. Scott hadn't spotted me, I was sure, and neither had the person in the 'van. . .

But I didn't want to risk being seen. . . being chased by two like Scott. . . the thought of what would be at my heels. . .

I waited until Scott was level with the lay-by, then turned and hurried home, glad for once to be back in the crowded centre of town, where people staggered home under boxes of groceries, or got caught in the five o'clock clog up. And other normal things. . .

Next day he came up to me, finding me without any difficulty in the doorway where I was huddled out of the blowy rain. It was early, and three bells hadn't yet rung—the signal for the duty teacher to let kids into the school.

"Hey," he began cheerfully, "want a sweet?"

Scott's hand came out of his pocket clutching a much delved-in bag of jelly babies. He took one himself, stretched the head between his teeth until it parted from the body, then popped the whole thing into his mouth. He offered up the bag.

I ignored it.

"You don't really expect me to carry on as if it didn't happen, do you?"

"Happen?" Some of the cheerfulness ebbed away from Scott's expression, like rubber easing back towards its normal position.

"You know what I mean—Gurney. . ."

His eyes drifted away, not quickly like startled insects, but with a slow heaviness, tired eyes. He nodded.

"I know. . . I tried not to let it happen, Nick, but it always does. I always go too far."

"Why?" I had to ask it, even though it felt something like the first crack in a dam wall.

"Dunno. Suppose because I think it makes people like me. You know. Everybody loves a clown."

"You can always see through a clown's tricks," I told him. "They're obvious and clumsy, been done a thousand times. That's why people laugh. You're just too good at what you do. . ."

It sounded all very philosophical, but I believed then that I was right. And I still do.

"You all kept at me to do it—you as much as anybody, Nick!"

I knew it, and dreaded to think what I might have asked him to become if I'd not thought to put the brakes on now, to put an end to it.

"My mum used to warn me about it—about giving too much of myself away," he went on in a quiet voice that sounded strangely final. "She said that I could be anything I wanted to be, but that above all else I was to be myself.

"Trouble is, no-one likes me as myself."

His smile came from far away, too deep and rich a mixture of self-pity and loneliness and defeat for me to sympathise with properly or even fully understand. I knew then that the big gypsy caravan out Draybrooke way was his home, and that soon he'd be moving on.

"Ah," I said, not wanting him to vanish thinking the worst of me, "you're not such a bad old stick."

I put out my hand towards his shoulder—and had it flung away by another hand that was big and square and bony.

Donovan stepped into view between us. He'd sneaked up along the wall and, for all I knew, might have listened to everything we'd said, though how much of the truth he'd guessed was another matter. He put on his shark's smile, the smile of the bully who has weaker kids at his mercy, and looked evilly from one of us to the other. Then he noticed the sweetbag that Scott was still holding, reached out and took it without resistance.

"What else you got?"

I began to relax away from the terrible thought that Donovan knew all about Scott and was ready to exploit it: even if he had listened, we hadn't given away the secret in so many words. . . The stupid prat was just after sweets and maybe money.

I played it casually, took the fifty pence I kept for emergencies out of my inside pocket, and gave it to him.

"You?"

Donovan's eyes swung towards Scott, who shook his head sort of dumbly.

"He's new," I cut in. "He doesn't know what you're after. . ."

"Money, cash. . ." Donovan held up his fingers and rubbed them together. "Enough of it might just save you from getting mashed, understand?"

It was quite likely that Scott didn't, because nobody would've been daft enough to say no if they did.

"Come *on*, I ain't got all day!"

Donovan's short-fuse temper flared up. He grabbed Scott's jacket lapels in his big knobbly fists and swung him round against the wall. I began to rummage for more coins. . .

Then it happened, suddenly and frighteningly. Scott's face seemed to blur: I got the impression of skin flowing over bones that dissolved and coagulated, changing and reforming like time-lapse pictures of clouds. A shark's smile swam to the surface of that sea of change.

"Come *on*, I ain't got all day!" Scott said in Donovan's voice, although now he had Donovan's face too, right down to the scatter of blackheads across his nose, that still swirled into place like specks in stirred milk.

Donovan grunted in surprise, began to scream and move away.

A hand rose up, Scott's hand. It was as big as a dinner plate, as big as a dustbin lid. It clamped octopus-like over Donovan's screaming face, cutting off the noise.

It made me sick, to see a hand that size holding a boy's head

29

like I'd hold an egg. . . Don't squeeze, Gurney, I thought-begged: please, don't squeeze him. . .

But Donovan had fainted. He sagged in Scott's massive grip and dropped. We'd won.

But we hadn't got away clear and free. Other kids were about now, with just ten minutes to go to the bell. Some had stood watching, a couple of them fourth years, a couple of them fringe members of Donovan's gang.

One of them called, alerted others. They all came running.

"Inside!" I shouted at Scott, eager to get him away—though not worried about what the gang would do to *him*. . . At the same time I battled with the door onto the corridor—stuck firm, bolted shut.

"Out of the way," Scott said—thankfully Scott again except for that awful hand, which clenched like a club and smashed easily through the six-mill wired glass to reach the bolt at the top.

Scott yanked the door open and dived through.

We ran, meeting no-one, although things were more serious now. Children were shouting and yelling outside: I heard the duty teacher blowing a whistle to shut them up, attract their attention. . . Soon he'd learn all about Nick Green and his weird friend, his monstrous friend: then the whole school would be alerted, the police called. . . Scott wouldn't last the morning.

At the end of the long empty corridor we stopped. My heart was bumping and I heaved in breath. The echoes of shouts banged about the walls behind us, catching us up.

"You've got to get out Scott. I mean, away from the school."

"Don't worry about me," he said, very calmly, just as if this was run-of-the-mill stuff to him. And it probably was.

"What'll you do?" I wondered. He was about to tell me, too, when the air crackled and a hunched shape appeared up at the French Block end.

"Gurney! Green! Come here *at once*!"

Meres, scuttling towards us, infuriated no doubt by the shattered doorglass and all the fuss we'd caused.

"Move it Scott." I pushed him on. Half way down the corridor the first bell went, shrilling over our heads. We were opposite the bio lab, another locked door, but kids were starting to appear at both ends of the corridor, with Meres' ghettoblaster voice herding them before him like sheep.

This time Scott didn't hammer through the window. His right hand moved towards the keyhole, fingers pointing, lengthening ever more delicately. Three fingers slid right in, twisted and clicked the lock open. His mum was right—he could be anything he wanted.

He pushed the door and stepped into the lab. I made to follow, but he stopped me.

"No point, Nick. You're in enough trouble already. Anyway, I'm leaving now. You won't see me again."

"Not—see you?"

"Well, you won't recognise me, OK? Leave it at that."

I nodded stupidly, trying to catch my breath, say goodbye, explain how I felt, all at the same time and in the few seconds before Meres reached us. I didn't manage any of it.

Scott put out his hand and shook mine. It startled me to feel that hand—ordinary, warm, human.

He turned, looked quickly around at what there was, and began to *change. . .*

Two seconds later Meres caught me, nearly choking me as he grabbed my collar and dragged me back.

He barged into the bio lab—into silence and stillness, with a hundred eyes watching him from preserving jars and the locust cabinet and the fishtank.

"And *where* is that *friend* of yours?" Meres thundered, attempting to wither my soul.

31

I shrugged, all innocence, too dizzy with amazement to be scared of the man.

"I don't know sir," I said, with absolute truthfulness.

I ran all the way to the lay-by that night, and as I expected, the caravan had gone. And I have never seen Scott since, though of course he said I wouldn't.

All the same, it's not easy to take the world for granted any more, and I look with new eyes at the stones and the trees, at the birds, at the sky. . .

Catch

Reg Button didn't care about anyone much. Which was why I loved him. He was old long before I was born, most of his life spent in a past that I had never seen and could hardly imagine. His wife had died fifteen years earlier, children grown up and moved away. He had a house and a pension, some money put by and a lot of empty time left to him.

We became friends not because he saw himself mirrored youthfully in me, nor because either of us went out of his way to be sociable. It was simply that he liked solitude and so did I, and on a cold, late September day at Pitsford Water, neither of us expected to meet a soul.

I'd come down to the reservoir to get away from people; a bossy sister, irritated snappy mother, a Saturday boss who expected you to do a paper round for peanuts and thank him for it. . . Besides, things hadn't gone too well that week at school. I'd fancied my chances with Anna, took a week to build up the guts to ask her out and then had been stared at as though I'd caught green measles. Great eh, especially when later in the day I'd seen her with Royston Simms—a kid with about as much personality as a warped plank.

I decided to walk the three miles out to Pitsford, following the old railway cutting most of the way, as far as the bridge (no longer there). *And* the tracks have gone, taken up for the metal: even the gravel's been scooped away for re-use. Not that I mind, because the land has been left to settle back into itself, become natural again.

After dawdling through the piles of bramble, stopping every few yards to guts a mouthful of fruit, I got a move on to arrive at the water before one. I'd come to catch fish—not 'to fish', that was about as boring as I could imagine, but rather to pick up the few trout I wanted as quickly as possible and spend the rest of the afternoon thinking, dozing, watching the grey rippling flatness of the lake, like dull planished iron in a wind that had something of autumn in it.

I reached Pitsford with time to spare, turning off the top road into the lane that took me through the village (a post office, a pub and six houses) to the great open grass slope that swept down to the waterline.

I went straight to my favourite spot, a deep clear backwater pool half hidden by rocks. It was fed by a stream draining off the hill, the water tumbling whitely off pebbles. Trout liked to gather there, enjoying the fresh, aerated water with its boil of bubbles. Maybe the movement of it made them sluggish or dazed, because it was always easy to prod them with my two bits of dowel that had onion netting stretched between. After drifting reluctantly a while, the fish seemed to guess they were being hunted, and turned to swim for it, straight into the mesh. I'd haul them out, bash their heads on the rocks to kill them. And that would be that.

Course, it was not allowed even though I had a licence to fish the water, and no-one would ever call it sporting. But I didn't do it for sport: I did it to eat trout.

The reservoir was slightly choppy, with a few distant boats out, like slivers of drifting white paper. I cast a glance round to make sure nobody was nearby and watching, then stooped to net my first fish. . .

It was easy. I caught a big two pounder within five minutes, hauled out a second slightly smaller one soon after, and was busy stalking a third. That would be enough, no point taking more than I wanted.

I saw the shadow over the water and heard the voice at the same time, and nearly jumped in with the shock.

"That takes me back, though I used ash-sticks and not them fancy bits o' stuff you got. . ."

I whipped round, both guilty and angry at once. The old man was standing on the high bank to my left, with the cloudy grey sky beyond: I had to squint to look at him properly. . . and he looked like a fisherman: great baggy cord trousers and canvas-lined wellies, a big green waterproof that crackled when he moved, tackle box slung round one shoulder and his rod, all packed up, hanging by its strap from the other. Damn! Just my luck. Now he'd fetch the water bailiffs out and that would be that.

At least, that's what I expected. But he simply stood, and watched, and I thought to hell with him. I turned back round to fish for my third trout.

"You used to do this, then?"

"Oh yes, years ago. Matter of necessity then. Not for you though. . ."

"No."

"Do it for sport?"

"No, for the taste of trout."

He chuckled at that, a sound worn smooth in his old throat. "Best reason there is," he said, and: "My name's Reg Button."

"Steve Haynes." I broddled about with my sticks in the water for a moment longer, but I was getting stiff. When the third fish turned its heavy hammered-lead body aside from the drifting net, I stood up with a grimace. Reg Button was smiling, his face all lines and creases, and suddenly it occurred to me that he didn't really look like a fisherman after all, but like something else that I couldn't put my finger on.

"You like trout too?" He nodded and I picked up the bigger fish and told him to stuff it away in his box pretty quick.

"Thank you son. Saves me the bother. You'll share a spot o' lunch wi'me?"

"OK," after a slight hesitation. "I've got nothing else to do."

We sat on the grass slope some way from the rock pool and Reg delved into his box for a bag of sandwiches. The food was wrapped, but I made a face when I saw the Tupperware box rustling with maggots that he kept right next to it.

"They for afters?" I asked with a sickly grin.

"Lovely spread on toast," Reg answered with no trace of mischief in his eyes. They were blue eyes, pale, like a long-ago sky, and the whites of them had gone a bit yellow and wet. He had a big bulbous nose with burst purple blood vessels at the sides. I made a bet with myself that he used a huge red spotted handkerchief to blow it.

"Here." He handed me a wedge of sandwich, two thick roughcut slices of brown bread stuffed with yellow cheese and tomato. It was a man's sandwich with nothing delicate about it.

"Don't you cut the crusts off?" I asked him in mock surprise. He smiled and his eyes twinkled as if to say 'stop yapping, start eating.'

We tucked in.

Afterwards Reg shared his two-pint flask of tea, the strong brown liquid making the roof of my mouth feel like fur.

And we talked, endlessly, which was ridiculous, because an hour earlier we had been complete strangers: now we swapped yarns like old friends. I moaned on about school, petty problems really, and grumbled about my mum and dad. Reg listened without saying much, nodding occasionally in a way that did not imply agreement or disagreement. Sometimes he spoke about his childhood: it sounded sepia, faded and faraway. Reg's voice was thick with nostalgia, a kind of longing for summer afternoons that would never come again.

"Well," I said, my voice lazy in the thin sunlight that had made the afternoon as warm as it was going to be. "I've never much bothered about the past. It's gone. What's done is done. . ."

"But what's never done remains undone," Reg said. I made my mouth screw up.

"Come again?"

"The past is full of lost potential. Most people have wasted their lives. Perhaps I've wasted mine. . ."

"I hope you're not suggesting I'm wasting mine."

Reg said nothing. I looked round too late to see him nod or shake his head.

"So, not keen on fishing?" he said after a silence.

"Not much."

"I'll show you fishing." He stood with a grunt. I followed him, shivering a bit now because the sun was close to the trees and the wind off the water had turned chilly.

I asked him, "You live close by?"

"In Pitsford. Why, you got to get back home Steve?"

"Naa," I told him. "I've got all the time in the world."

Reg's house was maybe the biggest in the village, an old three-storey Victorian redbrick with brown and green rooftiles and light blue paintwork now peeling. A tatty yew hedge ran the length of the frontage and down the side. The place loomed. It was not as neat and trim as the other houses in the village, but looked lived in and a bit scruffy round the edges. Like Reg himself. I took to it though, as I had taken to him.

He made some sort of mumbled apology about the state of the garden: didn't look too bad to me with its limetrees still brightly in leaf, well-used plot for vegetables, and grass summer-long September-golden: the sort of garden where little kids never tire of adventures.

We went inside to a hallway that smelt of sweet tobacco

37

smoke. And the same smoke seemed to have stained the light honey-coloured. There was a tall coatstand with a place for sticks and umbrellas, a mirror, and a small round table. I stood and stared. On the table was a green bronze dragon, a foot long, wingless, lizard-back arched aggressively. It was beautiful.

"Chinese, from the Chou Dynasty," Reg was telling me. "Nearly two thousand years old as far as I can judge."

"It must be worth a fortune."

"Probably. . ."

Probably! I nearly dropped where I stood. The old duffer had to be cracked to leave something lying about unprotected on his hall table like that. And hadn't he got it valued?

But now he was hanging up his waterproof, beckoning me into the front room.

The place was a museum, cluttered with glass cabinets and display cases, boxes piled high in the corners, drawers roughly labelled with faded embossed tape. . . The room was dark with heavy curtains pulled half across, but despite the gloom my eye caught the grey gleam of weaponry, swords and knives, the white shine of bones, the dull distorted paintings of past ages hung on the walls.

It might of course have been forged or cheap reproduction stuff, but somehow I doubted it. I had begun to know the man, and that told me this vast miscellany of objects was real.

"This is amazing, Reg," I said quietly. "Never seen anything like it."

He hum-hummed a bit with pleasure and showed me one of the swords.

"No," he said as I started to admire it, "not a sword. It's a scramasax, single-edged longknife used by the Anglo-Saxons. This is one of the bigger sorts. You can get them as short as nine inches. Look at the handle here, gold inlay, beautiful workmanship. One of my better catches."

That's when I began to feel cold prickles up and down my neck. I'd thought Reg might have been eccentric, up until now. But the way he was talking made him crazy or—or else something was happening that I could hardly imagine.

Reg leaned the sword—the scramasax—against a drab 'forties double wardrobe and picked up an oval lump of bone about twice the size of a hen's egg. It was a carving, crude but powerful, of a girl's head. The features were simple and smooth, sort of innocent. Reg smiled distantly as he handled it, turning the thing over and over in his hands. The skin of his palms was as shiny and brown as onionskin.

"It's a portrait, one of the earliest you'll ever find. Cro-Magnon sculpture was rare, and most of it was religious. This is probably a sister or a daughter—"

"Where'd you buy it?" I asked, almost aggressively.

"Found it, son. A long cast, this was, and a difficult one."

"Where, Reg, where did you find it?"

"Let's go fishing," Reg said.

I followed him out of his room of treasures into the hallway again and up the stairs. The light was going now, just deep red puddles of it in corners and strips of it on walls. The house seemed to be bigger, less friendly, and I felt we were walking deeper into strange and hostile territory.

A half open door at the end of the landing showed me Reg's bedroom (stuffed with more of his priceless junk), but we went the other way, to a room at the back of the house.

This place looked less well cared for: landing carpet was threadbare, floral wallpaper dull and faded. The air smelt— not fusty, but not far off that, kind of old: an earthy smell.

And I could hear the sound of the sea.

"What is that, Reg?" My voice came out hardly above a whisper. Reg answered me by pushing open the big pine door of the back room. Night had come, or maybe it had never left. The room was very dark, and chilly with air that moved steadily in a strong draught across our faces. Here the sound was much louder, a huge and distant crashing of wave over wave, of breakers churning pebbles on an unseen shore.

"I'm scared Reg. . ."

He put his hand on my shoulder, a heavy and calming hand. When he spoke his voice had changed: now he was like a kid again about to open presents on a Christmas morning.

"Don't be. Just take some care Steve. Now, two steps forward—that's it. See what's there. . ."

I strained to see. The darkness was not quite complete. Looking back I noticed a pale fan of natural light sliding in under the door, now shut, but besides that some far and faint illumination was in the air around me. And by it I could pick out a clutter of objects scattered in a ragged line on the bare floorboards at my feet; some sticks and lumps of soil, bent scraps of metal, a Coke bottle, other stuff I couldn't identify. The floor faded beyond this into darkness.

Reg squatted down and picked among this flotsam like a beachcomber, muttering or grunting to himself in disappointment, disgust—then some excitement.

"Here's something." He scraped away a thin crust of grey mud with his fingernail to reveal a small imperfect disc of dull yellow metal. He pressed it into my hand.

"Souvenir. Roman I think, by the ear of corn symbol. Anyway, keep it safe."

"What's going on here?" It wasn't that I was scared any more, just curious now, beginning to get caught in Reg's excitement. He chuckled.

"You've got imagination enough to guess. Sit there, cross-legged is best. Are you cold?"

"Not really."

He walked a few steps away and came back with an ordinary fishing rod and another tackle box, like the ones I had seen him with before, but not the same.

40

Reg sat beside me, checked for snags in the line, drew the rod back and cast out. The weight sailed into the night and the reel spun with a zing of uncoiling line. I heard no splash, but the line kept going, farther—farther into the depths.

"What," I asked him, "do you use for bait?"

He smiled. "None needed, though I've never pulled a trout up yet."

"You've fished for all those things downstairs?"

"Every one of them, but you can never tell what you'll haul out. For every bit o' stuff worth keeping, there's twenty things I throw back—"

"Back to where they came?"

"Probably not."

"Coins in coal. . ."

"Wha's that?"

"I read about it," I said. "People have found coins in coal that was millions of years old, and in 1961 in California, miners found what they thought was a sparking plug in a lump of fossilized stone."

"Ha, well I hope you're not blaming me? I don't suppose I'm the only angler along these banks. . ."

I thought then that maybe I'd offended Reg, for he said nothing more for nearly an hour. At one point he passed the rod to me and went away.

I sat in that nowhere-place, in the near-dark, listening to the sea that was not a sea, wondering what strange ships sailed out there and if they ever visited still backwaters like Pitsford—until Reg came back with two big white mugs of steaming coffee. He was saying sorry, and I said it too by drinking every drop.

We caught nothing that night except a rather modern looking bottle of green glass. I wanted to hang on to it, but Reg hurled the thing away.

"Useless rubbish," he said.

41

We never heard the splash.

After that, I visited the old man a couple of times a week. He always showed me some more of his treasures and any new finds, and then we'd go to fish. The winter drew on and so I never saw the back room in the daytime, and I think I never wanted to, for I feared it might still be as black as midnight.

One time I asked him, "Why'd you do this Reg? Not to get rich. . ."

We were both muffled up in duffle coats and gloves, scarves and woolly hats. The cold was cruel and our breath smoked in the air. The sound of the waves was fiercer tonight, wilder. Out there—wherever it was—must have been winter too.

"Nothing to do with money. Why do fishermen sit their Sundays away in any case? They like to catch, but thinking about the catch is just as good. Besides, this is better. Because you never know what's going to come along. . ."

Reg was right about that. One night after I'd made about the best and longest cast of my life—and I was getting pretty good at it with all the practice—I felt the line stretch tight and the rod judder in my hands.

"Reg!" I called to him, panicking. "Reg—help me!"

I could feel some heavy, powerful thing thrashing on the hook, its wild movements communicated up through the line and the rod, which was now arced over like a rainbow.

"Reg!"

I screamed it. The thing was pulling, a terrible force, and I took a step forward helplessly. I'd stood up when the line had first tightened, but now I wished I hadn't. My boots gritted on gravel, slid an inch on mud.

"Reg. . !"

He came clumping over and with a swing of his heavy right arm he knocked the rod out of my hands. My grip had been frozen to it, clamped in a panic to the cork, and my mind had been frozen too, unable to give the order to let go.

42

"It was alive! Whatever it was. . ."

"The monster pike at the bottom of the lake," said Reg, grinning wickedly. I forced myself not to speculate.

I bought him a new rod and reel for Christmas, with my paper-round money. I'd been saving for a radio controlled car, but that didn't matter. It wasn't the most expensive tackle around, or the best, but he opened the package with tears in his eyes and blew his nose into a huge red spotted handkerchief. I smiled inside when I saw it.

"You're a good lad Steve. You know I could always have sold one of my treasures to buy the fanciest rod in the country. . ."

But we knew, both knew, that then it would have been just another rod.

For a quirky thank you, Reg took our photo together. He set up the camera, adjusted the shutter delay and hurried round to stand beside me, arm on my shoulder like a proud granddad. He had two copies of the snapshot made, and gave me mine just after New Year. I stared at it; no photograph had ever been like this one: not because this was different, but because now, to me, its moment had become as much a part of the past as the Pyramids or a fossil shell.

"Thanks Reg," I said. "I'll keep it for ever."

That was the last time I ever saw Reg Button. I was kept busy with schoolwork for a week—teachers always launch into a new term with great enthusiasm—and didn't get round to Pitsford until the following Sunday.

We'd had some thick and gentle snow on Friday: Saturday had been fine, but the Sunday saw a shift in the wind from the northeast so the day arrived in the middle of a blizzard that only let up well into the afternoon.

By five all the clouds had been swept away and the sky glittered with stars like cut glass glowing with moonlight. It was a full moon. Reg had said something about it affecting

43

more than just the normal tides of the sea, and I was vaguely worried as I trudged the last mile to the village.

The worry sharpened when I reached the front gate. Something was wrong. The house, normally bleak, now looked abandoned and empty.

I pushed through the snow piles and went into the house using the key that Reg had given me. When I shouted his name the house echoed with it emptily, but no answer came.

I banged up the stairs and ran along the landing.

It looked as if a storm had hit. Fragments of soil, tufts of grass, leaves and twigs lay strewn down the passageway. The old-fashioned bowl of a lampshade above the stairwell had smashed, its glass lying like curves of eggshell on the wornout carpet.

I walked into the back room and a blustery east-coast wind that swept sand grains up into my eyes.

The room was a shambles. Quite large chunks of wood, and fist-sized stones were scattered all about. One thick stump of a log looked as though it had been hurled into the wall beside the door, dislodging wedges of plaster. The sea roared. And at our fishing place Reg's tackle box lay overturned, and the handle and a two-foot length of his rod, snapped off abruptly: the top section, weights and line were missing.

I will never know exactly what happened. Perhaps the storm was too much and swept him out, or maybe that monster pike from the bottom of the lake came rising through the depths while Reg sat and dozed away his hours on the bank. He was a lone fisherman, no-one else there to help him that night.

I carry on, visiting two or three times weekly, letting myself in with the key Reg gave me. No-one notices, there are no suspicious looks or questions asked.

And there is always the chance that I'll find him again, cast up somewhere, or floundering in a limbo of nothingness. I'll keep at it until people discover that Reg is gone, and his house is sold, its cargo scattered. What a stir that will make in the papers!

I'll keep at it, though I've fished far and wide and deep. Sometimes I wonder if you can swim in this sea, or sail in it to summer afternoons I thought might never come again. But I haven't tried that yet, for the waters are dark and the tides uncertain.

Dragon's Egg

Looking back, I don't know which bit was stupider: falling in love with Hayley Masters, or ignoring Austin and his dragon's egg. I suppose I didn't believe in either quite enough.

It had been a warm early September after a grey washout of a summer: lots of county cricket rained off, a barren wasteland on the telly, and farmers complaining that their harvests would be down on previous years. Nothing memorable stood out from the great stretch of the holidays, and it was only on going back to school and into the third year that things started to happen.

One: I was picked for the first team, Belter the games' master deciding that I'd played well enough in house matches last season to qualify for 'a coveted position' on the left wing. He made it sound like I'd just made the England squad, but I let him pour on the praise as well, even though we both knew my talent was mainly aggressiveness and turning up reliably for training sessions. Still, it was better than a kick in the teeth, as my dad was so fond of saying. . .

Two: I befriended this kid called Austin Williams. Don't ask me why, because even now I couldn't tell you. He had a maniac of a little brother whose name was Manfred, and they lived together with a mother who was about thirty-six, but who looked fifty—father having packed off several years before when life, I suppose, crossed some sort of threshold into nightmare.

To be fair, Austin has always been a good mate since we

first sat together in our new maths group (set four), but his loyalty was sometimes cloying and his dreams so vividly envisioned as to be frightening.

He lived in another world, did Austin. The teachers told him that—often crossly—right from the start. You know how teachers go on. . . I thought it was one of their expressions, part of a kind of ongoing reprimand for scrappily finished work. But of course, Austin didn't care. I mean, if you exist with your head in the sky teachers must seem as ephemeral as clouds across the sun.

Three: I met Hayley Masters, and from then on my thoughts coalesced around the image of her face.

She was tall and, well, grown up for her age: intelligent and very pretty, despite the wire brace on her teeth, which would come off in a year or so anyway. And her hair was black, as black as winter midnights, and it came down to her waist: didn't just hang there, it swirled. It was alive.

I knew she'd noticed me during, I think it was, the second English lesson of the term. We were reading some book, and the phrase came up; 'She gave one of those taunting smiles that made him go weak at the knees. . .' Pretty corny stuff, but my eyes lifted from the book and I found Hayley looking right at me across the width of two tables. *Her* smile was not taunting, in fact it was barely there at all: but her gaze was dark and clear and I realised that sayings are often corny because they're true. I stared her out, seriously, until she coloured and looked away. But first contact had been made: she was inside my head.

I thought I could do nothing better than hang around at the school gates after last lesson and maybe catch her as she went home. A mate of mine said she was new in the town, moved up from the Isle of Wight during the summer.

"Get in quick, Kev: half the male population of the school's out for the kill."

I believed it too, and although I'd never gone in for rat racing where girls were concerned, the thought of my arm around Hayley's shoulder on the way to some disco, or walking in the park, made my heart pound harder than if I'd run a pitch-length and back.

So I leaned against the white gatepost in the forecourt and tried to look casual while crowds of neatly-uniformed and sparkly-eyed little first years milled around me.

Just my luck that Austin found me before Hayley appeared. There he was, standing right in front of me, face up-turned and a big crooked-toothed grin stretched across it. He looked like something put out for the bin-men: scraggy shirt all frayed at the sleeves and grubby around the collar, grey school trousers sewn with blue thread at the knees, and at half mast showing green luminous socks beneath.

"Kev. . . Hiya Kev. . . Kev. . ."

"Go and play with the traffic, Austin," I said without looking at him. Hayley had come out of the Art block and was crossing the central playground in my direction.

Austin tugged at my arm.

"Hey Kev, I want to show you a place—"

"Will you clear off!"

"I've found a dragon's egg—"

"Yeah, later."

I saw Hayley half turn as though someone had shouted to her. She paused, and Steve Connell strode up all macho and swaggering and—do you believe this?—carried her books for her!

"Damn," I said, outwardly cool above a rising fury. "Damn and. . . A what?"

Austin was staring vaguely in Hayley's direction, wondering what the fuss was about. "Dragon's egg," he repeated casually, and with an overtone of hurt pride. He held out a fragment of something for me to look at.

I took it from him, a scrap of what looked like smoothly milled aluminium about the size of a playing card, but roughly triangular, curved and with snapped and ragged edges. It was light too, and thin, but so strong that I was unable to bend or break it. Spots of dull yellow speckled the outer, convex surface.

"If you hold it into the light," Austin started to explain, then moved it himself, tilting the piece of stuff until the greyish colour shone matt-metallically and the gold speckles gleamed.

I was fascinated, more by the mystery of what the thing could be, rather than because I believed it was what Austin *said* it was. Maybe it was from some machine or other, but at the same time it was oddly *natural*; a strange cross between manmade and organic.

"That's only a bit of shell, of course." Austin was superior now, almost snooty. "I can get lots of those. What's really good is the whole egg I found with them. Whole and unbroken."

"Where?"

Hayley and Connell walked off together down the road. Faintly, just before they turned the corner, her laughter filtered back on the warm afternoon air.

"I'll show you," Austin told me, giving nothing away, "after tea."

It turned out to be Rowland's Wood, a straggle of oaks on a hillside about five miles out of Rossborough on the Lenton road. Although the day had been fine and sunny, hazy cloud had thickened steadily so that by six o'clock the sky was heavy and yellow with bluish thunderheads growing in the south.

We made fair time—even with Austin's skinny legs and pedalling on his sister's bike which was about two sizes too small for him. He kept up bravely, but we were both sweating at journey's end, an itchy, uncomfortable sweat in the dry pre-storm heat.

"It's private land," I pointed out. We propped the bikes against the hedge: not many cars came this way. "What were you doing here?"

"Often come here. At Midsummer and Hallowe'en. . . or whenever I can really. I like it. 'S quiet and nobody ever walks through the wood, no farmers or hikers or, you know, couples. . . It's like. . . part of the Old World: nothing to do with cars and science, or TV or towns. . ."

"Austin, my son, you are weird!"

"Yeah. In a past life maybe I was an alchemist or a wizard or something."

Or village idiot. I thought it, didn't say it. We followed a dried out twist of pathway about a hundred yards into the wood before Austin indicated we should strike off at an angle.

He broke through a screen of bushes and the light faded at once as the leaf canopy thickened over our heads. Our shoes crunched on fallen acorns. A whippet of branch swished back across my face stingingly, and in the distance the first thunder grumbled.

"This is stupid, Austin. We're going to get caught in the storm and drenched. Or struck by lightning, knowing my luck!"

"We're nearly there, at the middle. You don't expect dragons to make nests out in the open, do you?"

"I mean, the whole *thing's* stupid. Dragons don't exist. It's make-believe, Austin, get me?"

"Dragons are grey," he said softly. "At least, they are in Europe. Chinese dragons can be green or red: in Scandinavia they have a blue colour, like heated metal. They can eat fruits or wood like many other animals, but they like to crunch stones, especially if they have iron in them. . ."

And he was totally sincere, utterly serious about it all.

50

That's what frightened me—at least, I thought that's what it was, until Austin suddenly stopped.

"The centre of the wood," he said, cocking his head as though to listen. "Six ley lines cross here. It's a powerful node. Can't you feel it?"

I could feel *something*: the faint ozone-crackle of the air perhaps, or just the sheer stillness of the place. But he was right. Something. Something.

Just then the world blinked, a pinkish flash that washed out all detail and colour; lightning in a split second.

During the interval between light and sound, Austin moved quickly to a big old tree in front of us: its heart was rotten, the trunk split and filled with orange flutings of fungus. Erosion, or something, had exposed its roots like a handful of clutching fingers. Austin scrabbled between them, flinging more scraps of 'shell' about in a panic, until his body relaxed and gently, very gently, he lifted out his dragon's egg and held it up like a trophy.

This, I thought, was either the best practical joke ever organised, or he'd found some strange species of fruit or gall or whatever. Or he'd discovered the first ever (known) dragon's nest. Mrs Whiteside our biology mistress was going to be pretty amazed at this. . .

Austin smiled briefly, but as the wind rose to thrash through the topmost branches his face changed, turning serious.

"Dangerous now," he said, a breathy whisper. "Let's go back."

We ran, hurrying like a couple of thieves the way we'd come, taking advantage of gaps in the undergrowth and then the track leading to the road. Coming out of the wood was like stepping into a warm, dark room: sky shadow-black and bulging with evil clouds, the wind dragging willow-herb heads into drifts of fluff and sweeping leaves in the direction of town.

I knew something was going to happen—I guess in the same way that Austin could feel the nodal point of the wood. My first premonition.

Our bikes were where we'd left them, innocently leaning. I noticed that Austin's had a wire basket at the front, lined with screwed-up newspaper, as though he'd planned to bring back this treasure all along.

A fresh gust brought a warm splatter of rain, high-summer rain fat and oily—I flinched a moment before I needed to—

Flash and flash, forks of light that looked fleetingly like the oak roots where the dragon eggs had been. . . Or whatever they were.

Austin's thin shape seemed etched on the picture of the land.

Then he staggered, nearly dropping his prize. It was round, like a turtle's egg, beautifully formed and smooth. I was suddenly afraid he would drop it: afraid of what might come out.

I jumped forward, one hand steadying his arm, the other cupping the metally sphere. . . It was humming, ever so faintly, like an efficient motor.

"God," I whispered, "Almighty."

The thing was alive.

We got drenched, as I'd anticipated. We freewheeled into town through a sizzle of roadwater, went straight to my house and hid the egg under a pile of comics in my den at the bottom of the garden. Really it was a shed that none of the family had bothered using since we'd moved to the house three years before. I'd offered to clean it out and creosote it, and then maintain it if it could be my den. Neither Mum, Dad nor Sue argued. . . I even had a padlock on it now.

"It'll be safe here," I told him. "I've got the only key."

Austin nodded, but vaguely, like his thoughts were far

away; seeing things that normal people did not think about seeing. There was one kid in the fifth year who was a real UFO freak: kept spotting lights and saucers in the sky, and then went telling his (few) mates that an invasion was imminent. He had even hinted that *he* was a Martian himself, but this was a dark secret never to be made public. The fact that the whole school knew and strenuously avoided the boy hardly mattered. . .

But Austin was different. Despite all the names I called him he was not mad, nor the sort who'd do or say anything for attention, even if it took the form of derision. He was, to tell the truth, pretty ordinary—average, but when he day-dreamed, you wondered how real those dreams might be.

"I shall want to visit it," he said, telling me gently, not asking: "every day."

"OK." I even considered giving him the key, not wanting to be involved whether the whole thing was true or not.

"Every day."

"Yes!" I saw Mum watching from the kitchen window and wiped the expression of irritation off my face. "Fine. . ."

"Because," Austin went on, "I'll need to prepare. For the hatching."

Over the next couple of weeks I even managed to forget all about the affair on one or two occasions, usually those times when I was actively pursuing my conquest of Hayley Masters. The presence of Steve Connell was annoying. . . well, actually it drove me up the wall and round the bend, but the kid was too much of a creep to be a serious rival. Hayley, very coyly but with great expertise, played us off one against the other; never telling him outright to clear off, always cleverly avoiding my efforts to pin her down to a date.

She was waiting, I soon realised, for the next big occasion on the school calendar, the mid-term disco. Since I'd been at

Rossborough the dance had served as a late settling-in social and an early celebration of Hallowe'en—meaning that the heads of year and staff only had one lot of organising to do. But they normally made a good job of it and the disco was always a huge success.

It was also something of a showcase. People who went and were noticed were talked about, sometimes enviously, sometimes bitterly, sometimes fondly. The dance formed the big gossip-generator of the year. And relationships that survived for a week *afterwards* tended to last. Don't ask me why, but it's true.

I thought hard about how I'd fit with Hayley, and she with me, and I reckoned we were a good match. I'd had enough of one-week, two-week dates: Hayley was interesting, deep and still. I'd enjoy getting to know her.

Meanwhile Austin had been as good as his word, coming round daily to tend to his 'egg'. At first I'd go down the shed with him, watch him lift the thing reverently, almost soothe it with his hands, and listen to it.

I'd tease him, of course, I think through a mild embarrassment that anybody could be so intense about something that was supposedly myth and legend. One time I nudged his elbow and chuckled at his panic as the sphere rocked in his hands.

"Steady Austin, might be an unexploded bomb."

There was no temper in him, no sarky comeback. He simply looked at me and smiled, such a knowing yet veiled smile that it frightened me. I tossed the key to him, acting as casually as I could, and didn't go near the shed again.

September went out warm and windy, but the first week of October was cold, with plenty of rain. The term had settled, I dealt with schoolwork steadily, as it came, under no pressure.

It seemed no time at all before the air began to dance with talk about the disco, and rumours took root and grew—often alarmingly and sometimes disastrously. Connell began to hang around Hayley more frequently and more intrusively: I let him make an idiot of himself with his fawning, and held back, judging my time almost to the hour.

With four days to go, I caught Hayley at the end of school and made the invite. She knew as well as I did that my intention had always been to ask her, and I guess we both knew what the reply would be. But she hesitated, staring shyly at the ground: all part of the ritual.

"You know that Steve has already asked me. . ."

"Oh yeah?"

"Mmm. Four times." The hint of a smile.

"I'm only asking once," I said. Big talk, but my heart was racing.

"He said he'd come anyway, whether I go with you or not. . ."

"Steve?" Hayley nodded. "And are you? Will you?" I said, feeling tight in my throat. She leaned close, kissed my cheek. She smelled sweet and her lips were cool.

"I like you lots, Kev. I'll see you at the dance."

The time came round in a flash. I saved up from my Saturday job and, with Mum's help, bought a new pair of jeans which went great with my white wool pullover. I felt good all that week, sort of glowing inside, but not sure if it was a grown-up feeling or one that was very childish. I ambled through my work and didn't care for once when it came back C-graded or worse. . .

And the future felt stable, the thought of dancing with Hayley like a solid base on which my happiness rested. Beyond that? Well, you never know. But I had hopes. And dreams.

Friday drifted by, the school day seeming like a brief diversion between the excitement of getting up and the deeper anticipation of the dance.

I didn't bother to check things with Hayley. She'd given her word and she knew I'd turn up. We had an understanding, a good first step. And neither did I trouble to visit the school hall at the end of the day to look at the decor, which I had done in years past: I wanted it all to be fresh that night, gleaming and colourful: I wanted the whole impact to come at once.

By six o'clock I was ready, although no-one even turned up until seven at the earliest. Mum knew better than to fuss me after tea, and Sue knew better than to tease. She'd had important days like this herself, private days, because so much of your self was visible.

So I just sat in my room gazing out over the back garden, and the gardens beyond, and the sky which was a moving grey-black mass of clouds dragging its sheets of blustery rain. I stayed for nearly an hour, watching, thinking.

Close on seven Austin turned up, a gawky little figure in the green dufflecoat that was too small for him. He unlocked the shed and went in. The door slammed back in the wind.

It was almost difficult to stir myself at last, go downstairs for my coat and step out through the doorway. I had gone through sets of possibilities in my mind time and time again, planning aftermaths, so that actually setting out to achieve them seemed troublesome.

The wind swept up the house-side spitting rain in my face. The sky was already dark and streetlights were coming on. I called cheerio to the family in general, pulled the back door shut—and saw Austin frantically waving at me from the garden. I made exaggerated mimes of pointing at my watch, shook my head and set off. His voice followed me, a distant thing plaintive and small. Why the hell *now*!

I paused at the gate, struggling with the dilemma of what to do, long enough for him to come running up. He almost fell against me, panting, gulping air so that for a moment he could not speak.

"Trouble," he said at last. "It's hatching, Kev. Now. But. . ."

His eyes were like sparks, and the skin had stretched taut and white around them.

"But *what?*" Anger and apprehension mixed. I wanted to push him away.

"It can't manage by itself. We need help, Kev. Kev. . ."

"I've got to go. I won't let Hayley down—"

"Please!"

And he started to cry, a totally hopeless sound, blubbery sobs and sniffles. Just stood there. His nose started to run.

I ran back, swearing all the way, not caring if Austin was behind me or not: past the lawn that was now leaf-littered and scrappy, down the side of dad's veg patch and into the shed.

It was hot in there, hot like a blacksmith's shop, and it stank like one: cinders and hot iron. The egg rested on a bed of gently glowing sparks. Austin came in behind me.

"It's trying to get out, Kev, but can't. Not strong enough. Listen. . ."

Imagine a nail drawn down glass, a scrabbling of such nails. . . That was the sound, but somehow softer and quite weak. And under that, a small pig-like grunting mixed with a mournful keening very high up the octaves.

The dragon was inside, ready to be born, but not able to free itself. It was going to die in there.

I rooted about on a shelf and found the penknife I used for whittling: it was one of those expensive Swedish Army knives with lots of blades. I crooked open the stoutest blade, bent over the egg (it was like leaning your face above an electric fire) and tried to make a cut. The shell was harder than steel.

I tried again, this time looking for a fracture or some

57

blemish in the sphere. Sweat began itching on my skin. A drop of it hit the shell and faded.

I found the crack I wanted, used a newspaper to protect my left hand as I held the egg steady, and levered with the knife in my right. I had to use all my strength even to drive the blade further—and then suddenly it snapped and shot off into a corner, but a fragment of shell had also come away, leaving a half-inch hole: steam or vapour lifted from the interior, and in the darkness of the egg I saw something glowing. It was curved, textured like golden satin, a beautiful swirl of shades like the surface of a soap bubble. It was the baby dragon's eye.

That stopped me dead. To see it was not like looking at a human's eyes, or an animal's: it was neither, or it was both.

I stepped away. The eye vanished and a tiny black claw probed through the hole and picked futilely at the edges.

"It's no good, Austin. The thing's had it. *I* can't break that shell, neither can you. Neither can. . ."

"It's a dragon, Kev," Austin said without any trace of sarcasm or revenge, sensitive to the shock of my acceptance.

"It's just no use. It'll die." I shrugged and handed him the knife.

I went outside and let the wind bring me back, as though I had stepped into a pool of icy cold water.

I was late to the dance, over an hour late because I had not run straight there. Instead, I'd wandered around the long way, through estates and the town centre rather than cutting across the rec. Everybody was there of course, and chart music bumped and clattered above the sound of laughing, chattering groups. Hayley was there. Her eyes were searching, though when I walked in she turned straight to Steve, giggled overloudly at some no doubt stupid comment he was making, and completely ignored me. Steve took advantage of her mood to drape his arm over her shoulder and nuzzle into her neck. . .

And she has ignored me ever since. I hung around for ten minutes, magnetically caught between pleading with her and taking Steve outside to mash that inane smile of his. . . I did neither. I hurried home and went straight down to the shed.

Austin had left. The place stank like an old bonfire, though there was little trace of damage. The air was thick with staling smoke and a mildly sulphurous tang that was both tasted and smelt, a little of each.

Dragon shell lay scattered on the floor, together with droplets of liquid, heavy and scarlet, metallic like mercury. I thought about cycling out to Rowland's Wood, where maybe Austin had gone to bury the stillborn thing, or perhaps to release it if. . .

He never told me, one way or the other, nor even speaks much when I'm around. He still looks distant and vague, seeing what is not in front of other people's eyes. Hayley and Steve are into deep and lasting relationships. . . Neatly sewn up. . .

And me? What was plain and simple, clear and easy to understand, is not so now. I deal with schoolwork steadily, as it comes, under no pressure. Days go by, as they used to. . .

But the difference now is that I don't know what to look for: a tilt of black hair at the school gates, or a gleam of metal-grey wing in the moonlight.

The Forever Man

Everybody knows that old empty houses are haunted, and the one in Patchley Woods was no different. It was a lost house in a forgotten wood. Well, forgotten, except by the town kids who sometimes went up there, mainly in the summer. No-one around at autumntime, except me, Daz and Simon —and they'll all tell you at the High School that we're crazy. . .

The fact is, I like spooky places, windblown nowheres full of cold wind and loneliness. Sounds odd, eh? Point is, people get on my nerves. They love themselves, love talking about what *they* do right, love grumbling about everyone else. It's so boring, you wouldn't believe. They're all like that at Kenniston, living in small circles, making no mark on life. I guess it's the same in your town?

I know, what's so great about me? Nothing, and I don't pretend there is. I just keep out of the way and dream my dreams, and wonder about the things that most people never worry over—

Like why Patchley Woods is so deserted, and why the old Lodge stands there in the middle of it with no path leading to the front door and none going from the back. Maybe the fact that it would cost a fortune to renovate has something to do with it. And who'd bother? With the new bypass around the town, no-one travels through Kenniston any more. Truck-drivers hauling freight from the east coast ports to the Midlands thunder by without glancing at the signs: reps head for the bigger towns with a bit of life: tourists go north to the Peaks or south and west to the Cotswolds.

Kenniston, deep green backwater in a busy stream, everyone living circles. Me, a bit bored, a bit angry, trying to hope that life is bigger than I see it. . .

Oh yes, and Daz and Simon.

Well, Daz—Darren Phipps—is a boff, a real brain. Kids hate him because he's clever and he will Go Far. All the teachers tell him that: Oxford, Cambridge. They've practically awarded him the degree already. But he's not God's gift to women, if you catch my drift: ears like radar dishes, freckles that almost join up to make one huge freckle, and these thick-lensed glasses that give him a real mad-professor look. Whoever marries Daz will do it for blind love—unless of course he makes his fortune, which he's quite likely to. He's the sort of kid who'll invent a starship engine the size of a walnut, or something.

Then there's Simon Greaves. Not a lot to say about him. He's a shadow in everybody's world picture, a thin grey kid from the children's home: looks as though everything's been drained from him. Kids keep telling him he belongs in a Dickens novel, whatever that means. He cries if he gets cold in winter: about as much strength in him as over-boiled cabbage. Simon is as lonely and empty as the places I like, so he tags along with us two because we tolerate him. He's the closest thing to a ghost without being dead that I can imagine.

It's an odd partnership, the three of us. I suppose if the truth was out we don't make one complete person between us. All weird in our own ways. It's how I want it.

I'll tell you about the woods. First, there's acres of them. I mean, you could get lost there all day and eventually find your way out late at night with the moon up. It's happened. I don't know who owns all that land, and I don't know who *knows*. The person who owns the Lodge must do, but that house has been empty longer than I've been around. I even checked up in the town library once, because the man who built the house must have been important to Kenniston: wealthy, influential, a merchant or a banker or something. No record. The librarian didn't know such a place existed, and threw me out when I started giving her some lip.

The house is the centre of the wood, its heart: protected by it, hidden by it. Great stretches of beech and some oak fill the head of the valley between the two A-roads that strike out north-west and north-east from Kenniston. And somewhere in there lies the Lodge. Can't tell you exactly where, no path. But it's there. All private ground of course, signs and rusted barbed wire everywhere. But who takes any notice of them? Besides, three kids wandering don't hurt anybody. Keeps us out of trouble round the estates.

After the long summer holiday came the long autumn term. By October the gold had spilled its way through Patchley and tarnished all the hillsides. There was a nip in the air by late afternoon, and evening followed quickly. Stars were out by eight.

Daz and Simon still came with me to the woods: along the torn-up railway line and then down the footpath that parallels the boundary of the Lodge estate.

We went a couple of times a week, when homework was light or there was nothing on the telly. Usually, I'd phone Daz and we'd haggle over a time to meet: me, I was ready to go at once, but that kid *always* had piles of reading to do, stuff about space or fossils or technology. I swear he'll need to stick a RamPac in his ear one of these days to hold all the facts. . . Then one of us would ring the kids' home and tell the warden that we'd call for Simon. The bloke didn't seem to mind. We'd always delivered him back on time before, and in one piece. Anyway, who really would have been heartbroken if he'd never come back one night? Some people have no real friends: some, like Simon, are luckier and can count on one or two. But these folk are half-faded out of existence in the first place, don't seem fully part of things. If life were a stream, they'd be flotsam. Simon was one of them.

It was getting on for the third week in October, I remember, and the prospect of half-term was now more than a distant point on everyone's horizon. Along with that time of year came Hallowe'en, Guy Fawkes', then the darkening tunnel of weeks towards Christmas.

There was a lot to get excited about, but the three of us still did not care to break our routine. On the Tuesday I arranged with Daz to go for a walk up to the woods, and we passed a message to Simon in maths which, luckily, was not intercepted, otherwise we'd have landed in detention.

So, it was organised. At home I stuffed down a quick tea, scribbled off my English essay—some stupid yarn about a kid who wakes up with magic powers—and walked round to Daz's place: it was uptown, you know, where the BMWs sleep cosily in their integral double garages and daddy rakes the leaves off the swimming pool each weekend. Amazing, isn't it, that half a mile away Simon was waiting for us in his jumblesale jacket, not really caring whether he ever went back to his home or not.

"You're in a rush," Daz said, matching my fast cruising speed through town with a ridiculous bumpy jog of his own.

"I want to get there while it's still light—plenty of time for your stargazing later."

Daz had brought his binoc's, a pair of Zeiss 7×50s, the best for the job.

"By half-nine Aldebaran will be well up," he told me happily, "and the Pleiades. But I really want to catch Jupiter if I can—"

"Catch Jupiter. . ."

"What?"

"Nothing," I said, irritated and not knowing why. "Let's get a move on."

We picked up Simon and made for Patchley: he trotted behind like a mongrel stray, not going anywhere special, but perfectly happy to be with us.

Daz demanded a rest half way there. We'd climbed a bit and left the town behind and below. It was a dark sprawl of buildings, few landmarks recognisable, still busy in its bed of streetlights. The woods formed a darker smear across the skyline, and above them the sky glowed blue and violet, and a single star shimmered fit to shatter.

"It's Capella," Daz confirmed for us: Simon was rubbing stiff calf muscles. "Fourth brightest star in the whole sky."

"Great," I said. Daz shook his head.

"Doesn't it interest you?"

"Knowing its name doesn't. But the fact that it's there is amazing."

No point trying to out-logic Daz: this was simply the way I felt. We stared at the star a while longer—it looked like the broken fragment of a prism—and moved on.

The atmosphere changes as soon as you walk into a wood. Even this late on in the year, when trees are starting to lose their leaves, enough of a canopy remains to make the air cool and still, and to shut out the noise of the world.

We used our regular gap in the barbed wire fencing, squirming through a screen of hawthorn bushes whose crimson fruits stood out brightly in the gloom. The soil was loamy, moist and scented—but messy. I slipped almost at once and put my right knee to the ground. I could feel the wet seep through instantly, and these were my second best jeans.

"Damn it. . ."

Simon giggled behind me. It'll be your turn soon, I thought maliciously.

We spent twenty minutes wandering. I love to soak up the

atmosphere. Daz did his usual and picked up acorns and leaves and other bits of stuff.

"You must have piles of this junk at home."

He nodded.

"Hey, shovel in the leaves through the window, shovel out the compost through the door!"

"Very funny Rob," Daz said. It was too dark to see if he was smiling.

"You got a torch?" I asked. I knew Daz had, in his collecting bag. I heard him rummaging and then the light dazzled us all—

"Turn it out!"

"God Almighty Rob," Daz said in a whisper, "I swear I haven't turned it *on*. . ."

As he said it, I realised that it was true. This was not torchlight, but rather a huge flood of brilliance washing through the wood. The light was everywhere, making the shadows of the trees look as black and solid as the trees themselves.

"Close encounters," Simon said pointlessly, making a little sound that was either chuckling or crying.

We dropped down into an undergrowth of ferns, just in *case* Simon's comment had substance, and crouched there very still.

"It's coming from the house," Daz murmured after a moment.

"There's no electricity at the house. . ." And Daz looked at me as if to say, don't be so naive.

The beam—or whatever it was—held steady for maybe three minutes, a soundless, numbing bluish light that must have had kilowatts or even megawatts of power behind it.

When it blinked out—again without a sound—Simon gave a cry of shock and we were all left with green after-images of trees standing in a purple night.

"Stay still," I warned, feeling dizzy and disorientated, "don't run yet."

I wondered why I myself felt like panicking. We'd not been hurt or even threatened, not seen anything except that incredible brilliance. Electricity Board, secret military testing station, starship from far corners of the sky, something worse?

It might be anything, I told myself, then checked that: no, it was nothing normal. I knew why I wanted to run. . .

There came a sound, again from the direction in which we judged the house to be. This time it was identifiable, the crush-crush of someone coming through bracken, the thumping of heavy footsteps on packed earth. But the pattern of the steps was odd, more like a horse's brisk cantering than a man moving.

"Let's get out of it," Daz said, the words breathy and trembling in my ear. "I don't want to know what that is—"

"Not even the name of it?" I kicked back pettily, but I knew how his stomach must be churning. The urge to bolt was strong, but squatting here quietly was the only control we had over the situation. Once we broke cover and pelted for the fence we'd have no more choice in the matter, and our presence would be known.

So we waited on. I had my hand clamped to Daz's shoulder to stop him darting like a rabbit: Simon leaned across and grabbed hold of my jacket hem. We felt safer for each other.

The sound of movement never vanished entirely. It ebbed and flowed through the woods as though whoever was making it didn't know the way out. Sometimes the clumping faded almost away, but then might come a heavy crash, branches lashing this way and that, the snap of wood, then the drumming again as the horse searched for a different route to freedom.

That was it of course! I almost slumped with relief. A horse from one of the local hunt stables must have broken loose and come blundering through Patchley in a panic: the lights were most likely from a Land Rover: men must be all around us trying to catch the animal, trying to stop it bolting; and hurting itself. . .

There were lights again, not the single blistering blaze of a searchlight, but coloured sparkles spiralling deep through the trees. Odd—car taillights maybe? A fire?

The reds and yellows seemed to gather themselves, then come hurtling between the trees with a fierce crackling that rasped and snapped in the air.

Against the whirlpool of sparks was outlined the shape of a man on a horse, riding dextrously, trying to keep to the shadows. But the shower of lights sped closer, moving now towards us.

"Where," Daz asked me, "is the horse's head?"

I nearly turned round and belted him, but what he said was true. I could see it now. There was no man, no horse, but a something that was both. A creature that didn't exist was galloping closer, trying to dodge a supernatural fire.

Daz strained to pull away. The man-horse grunted, leaped across a toppled bough and thundered past, speckling us with flecks of dirt and bits of stick. With a whoosh like a skyrocket the ball of sparks followed him, missed him and burst against a tree. For an instant the oak was made of gold thread and Christmas lights, sparkling like lacework. Then the darkness came and the soundlessness of night, and the air was charged with a dry metallic tingle of energy.

Now we stood awkwardly. We had stiffened into our crouch and it was painful to rise, like coming out of a shared impossible nightmare.

"Home James," I muttered, voice cracked and croaking, the humour in it leeched away.

We knew that the woods were not empty. What we had just

seen looked like a chase, and the man-horse thing had escaped.

"It was a centaur," Daz said, maybe following my line of thought. He came out with it as casual as you please. Stupid to argue with him. I knew what it was.

"Odd though. . ." Daz was babbling to himself. "Centaurs were supposed to be wise, kind, patient. They taught the Greek heroes to ride and shoot with a bow. . ."

"Maybe this one didn't get paid. . ."

Now we were quite close to the hedge, the fence, the open fields and the way home.

"Where's the gap?" Simon wondered. We dared not switch on the torch to look, so strained with our eyes.

"About—there—"

But someone was blocking the way. A man this time, an ordinary man, around my height: a bit scruffy looking, in a tatty green cord jacket, black trousers and muddy brown boots. There were twigs in his fairish hair, and he was holding one arm as though it pained him.

It jolted me to realise that we could see him: everything else was smothered out by darkness. And he could see us too.

"You boys. This is private ground."

"Yeah, we're just on our way out of it."

I thought the slightly laid-back, not-quite-insolent approach would work best, show him we weren't really scared, even though I wanted to pee myself desperately. Teachers normally responded to this one. . . But the man just stood there. Maybe he shook his head. I couldn't see him smiling.

He walked over to us and I gasped. He was just a man, not sinister looking or anything, and he was in a sorry state; face smeared with blood, skin pale and stretched, his dusty clothes were torn and frayed. . .

But he had the look of a king, and his eyes were as young as the stars.

68

"You saw it, everything that happened."

He was not asking us. It was as though our minds were glass to him. He just knew.

"We saw it," Daz admitted, probably wisely. If this character was mixed up in what we'd seen, there was no telling what he could do, though I saw no malice in his face. Perhaps I saw pleading.

"It is not safe to leave these woods yet. The creature you saw is still here, also searching for an exit."

"Can't he jump the fence?" The thought of a centaur trotting down Kenniston High Street suddenly made me want to giggle.

"The fences guarding this wood are not entirely made of barbed wire." He said this with a weary humour, gone again in a flash. "My defences are not perfect."

"Your defences?" Darren said. "You own Patchley, and the Lodge?"

"As far as it can be owned, I own it. I, er, manage the estate. . ." Once more the tired remnants of what had been a sharp wit and a bright sense of humour. I felt that this man was not dangerous to us, and that he needed help. He breathed out truth, already he was a friend.

"Can't we go home then?" Simon asked.

"Not yet."

And Simon smiled, like this was some kind of chance he had been waiting for. I pushed it further.

"But we can't stay out here, with that thing roaming, and you injured."

"I know. We must go to the house."

No-one argued, me least of all. The prospect of following the field path back to town while knowing what was out prowling was not a desirable one. Besides, in a strange way I was hooked by curiosity. Here was somebody who talked about centaurs as if they were an everyday sight. What else had he seen? And who was he? And why did he live in a derelict house? Material for my next English essay, I thought wryly: but classrooms and homework seemed a million miles away.

Of course, the house was not derelict, not with the man there to brush away the cobwebs of the illusion. True enough, the outer walls were crumbling and the windows were glassless black holes, and the smell of mould and rotting wood was rich in the air. . . But once inside things were different.

We went down a passageway. At first cracked stone tiles gritted under our shoes, and our footsteps echoed from damp walls. But as we went further the air turned warm, the walls grew smooth and new: around us like a transformation the house became well-maintained and lived in, this man's home.

For all that, the place was big and rambling. Some of the corridors were dark, obviously rarely visited: and curiously lit with a mixture of softly hissing gas brackets and electric lamps.

Finally we came to a big pine door, the bare wood glowing. The man pushed it open and led us through into a study.

I smelled books and old leather, sweet tobacco smoke and modern machinery: and again, that prickly electrical smell in the air that I'd first noticed in the woods.

"It's a beautiful place," Daz said, staring around as we all did. Bookshelves lined two walls and went right up to the ceiling. A third wall was taken up with metal racks of files, tapes, discs—and a stack of machines that was like a cross between the world's most sophisticated hifi and Mission Control at Houston.

Finally there was the man's desk, facing the window—a huge bay window with heavy green curtains pulled across.

"Amazing," Simon added. And I was impressed too.

Out of the dark, we became aware of the state we were in. My muddy knee seemed a bit pathetic, as we were all spotted with mud, our clothes soiled, jumpers snagged, hair wet, faces smeared. . . And the arm of the man's jacket was soaked in blood.

"That looks pretty bad," Daz said.

I agreed. "Shall we ring for a doctor?"

"That would not be a wise move. He would have difficulty finding a way through the woods, and what roams there might yet find an escape."

The man looked at me, I looked at him and it was like staring at a starlit sky. What had he seen to make his eyes so deep?

I shrugged. "We'd better do something ourselves then. Got some bandages?" I tried to sound casual but my stomach was rolling.

After a moment the man nodded towards a table that was littered with bits of apparatus, a microscope, books scattered and open, and an ornamental box. Daz went over, opened it and took out some bandages and antiseptic while Simon helped the man with his jacket and shirt.

The wound was deep and still bleeding. It was not a knifecut, but whatever caused it had been sharp, heavy and expertly used.

"The hooves of centaurs are not to be taken lightly," the man smiled, a thin stretched smile of pain. He knew as well as we did that bandages were not going to be of any use whatsoever.

"Which brings me," I said—loudly, to conceal the fact that I wanted to throw up— "to the sixty-four thousand dollar question: what are centaurs doing in Patchley Woods?"

Daz poured on neat antiseptic, then proceeded to make a botch-job of bandaging: but at least the wads of cotton staunched the blood and made the man more comfortable.

He went and sat down in one of his study chairs, his jacket draped round him. The room was warm enough, though I could see no sign of heating. We sat around him, Daz and Simon on the floor, while I pulled up his desk chair. It was like story time at school, only on this occasion I knew that we weren't going to be told make-believe. This was happening to us, and it was true.

"Imagine a frontier," the man said quietly, "bordering many lands. There are reasons why people remain in their own countries: reasons why some try to cross from one nation to another. Whether this is desirable or not, such frontier-posts must be guarded, and vulnerable peaceloving races protected from those that are strong and warlike. . .

"But I want to talk now of worlds rather than lands, of other places and times that in part do not even exist in this universe. These too have their borderlands, their frontiers: and these too have their refugees and their invading armies. Crossing points must be guarded, boundaries monitored and patrolled. . ."

"But who trespasses in Patchley Woods, except for kids?" Daz wanted to know. Either he was being abnormally thick, or sarcastic, and for once I really didn't know which.

I began to wonder. Maybe it *was* a man on a horse we'd seen, perhaps the authorities *had* been out—perhaps tracking down a madman who told stories of other universes. It made me feel cold. . .

The man smiled, eased himself painfully out of his chair and walked to the window. He took the curtain-pull and looked at us.

"Perhaps you are still not sure of me, not understanding that I don't talk of trees and fields, but of stars."

He drew open the curtains, then went over and switched out the lights.

The night outside was windblown and dark. And someone had lit a fire, for white sparks glittered through the trees and—

72

My perspective tilted sideways and spun round. I almost toppled forward, off balance and dizzied to realise that these were not sparks, but stars as the man had said: clouds of them, drifts of stars piled high against black nothingness. And the glow—that red bonfire glow was a much larger star, a sun nothing like our sun: it turned slowly and hugely into view, a faint cloud of shining gas like rosy veils of fog.

Then the vision was gone. The lights blazed back and washed out the sight—but not the memory of it.

Three of us stood there dumbstruck. Tears were dropping from Daz's eyes, not unhappy tears: and Simon looked as serious as I had ever seen him.

"So," said the man softly, "I speak true. You are the only ones on this world ever to know, though others have suspected, for occasionally a creature breaks through from another place and in time makes the folklore and legends of history.

"A thousand, or two thousand years ago I could afford to let them free. They were the persecuted of their own planets, the runners, the outcasts. They did no damage here and often greatly enriched Earth's cultures. But some come to destroy or conquer, and these I must send back. Besides, people have changed. The human mind is no longer open enough to treat them as your ancestors did."

"And the centaur is still on the loose!" Simon reminded us. The man nodded.

"Still free, still dangerous. And it is also true that the barriers surrounding this wood have been breached: I thank you for discovering the break by your entry, but that entry must be sealed. It could also make an exit. . ."

"We'll help you," Daz said eagerly. "Four of us could easily catch the thing. And, well, I don't know about the others, but this is the best adventure I've ever had!"

"These are not games I play." The man led us towards the

73

door. "I am grateful, but my concern is to see you safely on your way. There is much work for me to do, and the places I guard are not playgrounds. Go now: you may not be so easily spotted in the dark."

We went out into the night, the real October night with its high gusting winds that made the trees boom, and fast fleeting clouds, underlit orange by the streetlamps of the town.

We followed the man, not arguing, but heavy with the knowledge of what we had seen and the fact that we would not see it again.

"Careful now," the man said at one point. "I sense that the creature is near."

I felt exposed and frightened at the end of the line. Ahead of me, Daz trotted on like a little dog, while Simon held the man's coat-hem tightly, as a son would stay close to his father.

I shivered, not just because of the cutting wind, and listened hard through the crash of branches and whoosh of thrashed leaves.

The sound ebbed and flowed hugely, ebbed and flowed as the big autumn wind came rushing over the Midland plain, swept across the town and up the valley.

Then out of that sound rose the sharper noise of undergrowth crackling. A big, heavy creature snorted nearby—frighteningly close—and thudded out of darkness and tree cover from the left, plunging straight for us.

It was the centaur, could be nothing else, and its eyes winked like two gold coins spun in the air. We began to turn, reacting to its approach. Daz started to call out a late and pointless warning.

The man-animal reared up, chopping with deadly fore hooves. I saw the arch of its strong proud neck and glint of light on its white teeth: then I ducked as a hoof went cleaving overhead, churning into bushes and bracken a foot away.

The thing's powerful body spun and battered me over,

74

smashing me down. Daz too was on his back, Simon a short way off and diving for safety.

The centaur reared, breath whistling, shouting in a language that seemed neither music nor speech. But the threat was there, and the intention to kill us.

I rolled frantically, felt the thump-slap of the hoof driving into earth where my head had lain. The blow would have crushed my skull like a thin shell.

I tried to roll further, out of harm's way, and came up against a barbed screen of bramble. My jacket sleeve was caught, thorns already scratching through to my skin as I struggled.

And now the centaur reared again, towering, sure of the kill. I threw up my hand, knowing that it would be like trying to stop a train. . .

The night erupted silently, scalding away the dark in the blaze of white light that we had seen before. The creature flinched from it, the centaur's man-face showing anger and fear, its eyes flashing as red as coals.

"Scramble clear!" came the man's voice. I wriggled out of my jacket and dived, twisting round in time to see the light disintegrate into showering glimmers and sparks that ran along the outline of the centaur's body.

The sparks thinned, and as they did so the outline became vaguer, less clearly defined, until I could not distinguish it from the night. The high shrill cut glass cry of the centaur's defeat blended with the wind in the leaves and its presence with the cold loneliness of the woods.

I started to tremble, realising how close I'd been to dying. Daz nearby was wiping his face, trying not to show his little boy's terror.

"You OK Simon?" I asked.

Simon was standing beside the man, opening the front of his green cord jacket.

"Bleeding's started again. I'll help you back to the house. . ."

I expected the man to argue, but he didn't. After a moment's thought and silence, he handed Simon a small torchlike device—probably the thing he'd used to send the centaur back to wherever. And it seemed like more than just a casual gesture, an accepted offer of assistance.

· "Hey, Simon," I said, not thinking about it, "we'll wait for you by the fence, right?"

The two of them walked off through the trees into darkness. We turned and went the other way.

At the fence I scrambled through first, then held the wire for Daz to follow. I started off down the hill, hands jammed into pockets, shrugging out the chill.

"We said we'd wait," Daz pointed out. I turned, looked back up at him.

"Yeah, I'm sure. I just feel sorry I never said a proper goodbye, that's all."

There were questions and questions, suspicion at first and then a kind of resignation. Maybe the man's hand was in it somewhere, but no full-scale police searches followed, and after six months Simon's name was never mentioned except between Darren and me. Now I can't even remember what he looked like.

We still go to Patchley, the two of us, and wander about through the beeches and oaks. We've never seen the blinding light again or heard the night-time wails of things that were not foxes or owls: never found the place where that old house had stood lifetimes ago.

The Swapmeet

They met in the orange glow beneath a streetlight: Vaughn, Rick and Matthew, all with stretched smiles of excitement and eyes as bright as glass. It was late October, promising frost, and their breath smoked in the air. Another ten-week circle had swung round and it was Swapmeet Wednesday again.

Matthew spoke first, as usual. It was part of the tradition.

"All set then?" He casually switched his bike lamp off.

The others nodded, Vaughn with a greedy wink at his friends, Rick more cautiously as though (Matthew suspected) he was starting to grow sick of the adventure. But Matthew said nothing—not worth causing trouble before he had to.

"Come on."

They dismounted and walked with their bikes down School Lane, where there was less than a double armspan between the houses, along the cinderpath that bordered the waste ground, then emerging on the long gentle curve of Holland Park Road. The Swapmeet was always held in the big Assembly Rooms attached to the community college, and even from a distance they could see that the whole building blazed with light. It gave the evening a hazy, yellowish look: the cold air smelt of damp decaying leaves and, strangely, of metal: the boys' hearts pounded.

The time was just seven-thirty, but already the police had been out placing 'No Waiting' cones along the kerbs. All of the nearby sidestreets were jam-packed with parked cars, while more vehicles swept by dragging cold currents of air,

77

their brakelights dazzling as they came up opposite the main college gates.

On Matthew's initiative, the boys used a side entrance and wheeled their bikes round to the back, where they could shackle them by three lockchains to the railings.

"Don't want them getting pinched," Vaughn said, deadpan, and then began to snigger, faster and faster until the sound broke down into nervous laughter. Matthew grinned broadly, and in that moment Rick appreciated the differences between them. Vaughn was a short kid with straight, nondescript hair, a tuft of it sticking out from his crown. He wore glasses with thick black frames, and had acne. It gave his face an old, worn look. Rick imagined that Vaughn's appearance would not have changed in another twenty years.

Matthew was taller, handsome, somehow brighter—more alive with energy. He took great pains over his appearance: had his gingery hair styled regularly and chose his clothes to match its colour. Tonight he was wearing new blue jeans (not stonewashed because they 'had no style'), and a dark grey pullover beneath a silvery bomber jacket that had red racing bands on the right arm. A small white sports bag was slung over his shoulder.

But there was more to it than that, than just appearance, Rick saw. Vaughn was small in other ways—in his outlook. They all went to the Swapmeet to steal, and had done so since the first year of High School, yet while Matthew would turn up and carry out the plan by himself if necessary, Vaughn would never dare to. He was mean in his dreams, had no courage: Matthew's bravado seemed limitless. That and the cold seeping through the single layer of his denim jacket made Rick shudder.

Matthew led the way round to the front of the building where the sudden spillage of light made them screw up their

78

eyes. A huge white banner above the doors announced *Toy and Train Collectors' Fair Here Tonight.*

A few people had gathered, waiting to go in. Beyond the ticket table the aisles between the stalls seethed with the crowd, though the noise was muted as collectors inspected what was on offer rather than waste time in conversation. Rick could imagine how hot it would be in the room, his memory of past swapmeets being almost vivid enough to bring him out in a sweat.

"Three please," he said. It was his turn to pay. The woman at the table handed over a short strip of numbered tickets and a leaflet giving dates of future meets. Rick screwed the paper up and dropped it, those dates being carved already on his mind.

"It's as good as I hoped for," Matthew said in quick, confident assessment. The others agreed. The summer slack time was over, but the dealers had not yet begun stocking up with Christmas rubbish—new toys, mass produced and cheap that would appeal to the gift buyers and the little kids who came along.

In the boys' experience, the October swap was the best, with plenty of stalls in competition, most of them loaded with real memorabilia. The very rarest model cars and toys were kept behind glass, locked in cabinets, and this stuff was the cream; models like those didn't even have price tags on, and the old saying applied—if you need to ask the price, you can't afford to buy. Rick knew how true that was and usually gave the cabinets a quick glance only, moving away before desire and jealousy began to churn his stomach. Once, he remembered, he'd watched a dealer and a buyer standing over a one-only handbuilt Model T Ford, mixing quiet haggling with murmurings of mutual admiration about the quality and collectability of the car. After what must have been ten minutes of bargaining, both men nodded and the buyer took a roll of notes from his pocket. Rick watched with his mouth open as they were counted out, and stopped tallying once the three hundred pounds mark had been reached.

He'd had nightmares about the deal for a week afterwards, where the real monsters were the feelings he harboured towards the dealer and collector: envy, greed, rage, frustration. Soon after he'd told Matthew about it, and within the week Matthew had suggested stealing what they wanted but couldn't afford. Rick hadn't argued. The way he felt, it was either go along with Matthew's plan or give up visiting Swapmeets, and that he couldn't do.

The first time, when he was eleven years old, had been a nightmare in itself. Rick felt his face glowing hot with guilt all the time they were there, and on the way home he'd thrown up his tea into someone's hedge. But when Matthew dug into his bag and pulled out their catch, a warm melting of relief and comfort had spread through Rick's chest. Matthew handed over a one-thirty-sixth scale Oldsmobile Super 88 with metallic blue finish, tinted screen and yellow interior.

"For a good night's work," he said with a grin, and Rick believed him.

Then it was easy and the plans become smoother, more sophisticated. Vaughn joined the team early on and, although he showed no initiative himself, obeyed orders to the letter and could be relied upon to play his part. The anonymous look he had made him ideal for blending in with groups of people leaning over a stall-front, while he could palm a handsized model off a tabletop swiftly and invisibly.

The team worked well together, and their haul was always fat, the record on one memorable occasion—once they had totted up the price tickets—totalling eighty-nine pounds worth of toys.

"We could easily sell this lot back to the dealers," Matthew explained with malicious glee, thinking he was kicking back at a system that allowed some people to have so much and others nothing at all. They thought about that, but decided against it. After three years' successful operating, they each had extensive collections and had begun to specialise; Vaughn going for Minis in all their varied forms, Rick for space-related models, and Matthew for anything unusual and out of the ordinary. The prize of his collection was a silvery lead-alloy custom bike, a detailed sleekness of powerful engine and delicately spoked wheels. It was mounted by a skeleton whose rigid arms formed the front fork that connected the wheel to the rest of the machine. Two grotesque projections of bone from its shoulderblades made the handle bars.

"You could ride all night with the devil on that," Matthew had said laughing, "twice round the sky and then straight down to hell."

"It's hotter than I expected." Rick wiped sweat off his top lip and struggled out of his pullover, being careful not to stick his fist into any faces passing nearby. He had a bad feeling about this Swapmeet, something he could not explain, but which lodged in his head like a certainty. He said nothing, since it was an unspoken belief in the team that to mention bad luck caused bad luck, like the time they had almost been caught. . .

It had been a year ago, at the last October meet. Rick recalled that the weather had not been cold and crisp, but wet, dismal, and the chill of the air made your bones ache if you stood outside too long.

They'd come into the Assembly Rooms with dripping coats, feeling instantly itchy and uncomfortable amongst the packed crowd in the hall. Matthew scanned the stalls in his rapid but thorough way and decided they'd go for a set of World War Two hand-painted lead infantry models.

"We don't collect those," Rick pointed out, his stomach sinking: he saw Matthew's stubborn mood looming so made his tone reasonable, neutral.

Matthew's eyes went hard and angry.

"Never mind about that. I want something that's worth money, something we can sell back at another meet. I mean, look at that old duffer. . ." The three stared briefly at the stallholder. "Waistcoat, sleevebands, cigar. . . Who does he think he is? Do you know what his mark-up must be on those soldiers? He probably got them off some old pensioner for a fiver, *and* made out he was doing the poor sod a favour."

Matthew smiled, seeming to relax back into his determination to carry out the act.

"I want to *do* him, lads. I want to hurt him because he's loaded and because he thinks he's great. It's *him* I want, more than the boxed set. . ."

Vaughn nodded in his usual accepting way: Rick didn't, but went along with the plan anyway.

They used the haggling-under-the-table ploy, a guaranteed winner. It was a three-man gambit and the boys had worked out their parts to perfection long ago.

As the front man, Matthew went in and began to talk technical with the dealer. It took a lot of knowledge, but Matthew spent long hours between meets reading the collectors' guides and the old manufacturers' catalogues (themselves rapidly becoming rare and sought-after). Depending on the swing the conversation took, Matthew's tone would grow effusive and admiring, or angrily critical at the price of the item. Meanwhile, Rick would move up close as though listening with interest, hovering with the several other people invariably attracted by the banter. Vaughn, to create a diversion, would begin searching through the rummage boxes of old and chipped models to be found under most stalls.

At a given signal (usually a nudge with Matthew's foot), Vaughn would attract the dealer's attention and begin a quick barter for a handful of junk cars. Deprived of entertainment, collectors always began to drift away—and with them went Rick who had lifted the target model and stuck it under his coat or in his bag. The brief aftermath would consist of Vaughn buying a couple of cheap toys, and Matthew waving fond farewell—or making a sarcastic parting shot—with a comment like, "Well, I can't afford it anyway. . ."

That was the plan, tried and tested. And it would have worked again, if some little girl hadn't spotted Rick with the boxed infantry in his hands.

"Daddy, that boy hasn't paid for those soldiers. . ."

Rick felt his stomach tighten unbearably, and fat oily stars popped before his eyes. The team almost broke and ran for it—almost: the rummage cars dropped from Vaughn's numb fingers and he put his hands to the floor to support himself. Rick thought he was going to vomit in the haggle-box. . .

Matthew stayed calm. He threw the little girl a disdainful look as the dealer leaned forward in alarm and took the infantry set from Rick.

"He's only looking, dear—he couldn't afford them anyway. They must be worth a packet, right?"

The dealer told him how much, and Matthew's careful smile stiffened a little.

The three left soon after, out into the blanketing greyness and safety of the rain.

"Oh God. . . Oh—God. . ." Vaughn said on a shuddering breath.

Matthew chuckled. "Calm down. We got away with it didn't we?" And then they heard ice in his voice. "Bloody little kids—shouldn't be allowed into these toy fairs. . ."

83

*

Rick replayed the old movie of that night in his mind, prompted to it by the same sense of impending disaster. He even scanned around for the same waistcoated dealer, but the old man had not turned up.

"What's the plan tonight?" he wondered, hoping that Matthew would not detect his nervousness: thinking bad luck *makes* bad luck, he reminded himself.

"We add to our collections tonight. I've already spotted a couple of Minis, Vaughn—limited edition colours and racing trim. There's always space collectabilia about. . . And for me?"

Matthew smiled dreamily.

"I think it'll be something special. I feel it in my bones."

"Like what, Matthew?" Vaughn asked, not interrupting the sweep of his eyes across the laden toy stalls.

"Don't know—but then, that's half the fun. Come on."

They moved into the crowd, blending with it, appearing casual and quiet as they made their first circuit of the hall. The stalls were always arranged in a double ring, and the traditional route was around the outer circle first, then the inner. By unspoken agreement they earmarked the stalls they would work, either because the models they wanted were easily accessible, or because the stallholder looked the sort of person who would not realise that he was being robbed.

Usually, after the double circuit, the boys broke for a coffee and worked out their priorities and which ploys they would use. It was a safe and familiar routine that gave them confidence for the actual operation. Tonight they did not get that far.

Rick saw it first, a compact little table and some display shelves tucked away in one corner. The sluggish parade of collectors seemed to be passing it by, which was crazy—impossible, in fact, to Rick's way of thinking.

He touched Matthew's arm with a trembling hand. Matthew stopped dead and the three just stood and watched.

It was the stall they had all dreamed about, a kind of paradise for collectors, and especially for collectors who didn't want to pay. First, nothing was behind glass or beyond reach. All the models lay tantalisingly close at hand, and they looked brand new, even the ones the boys knew to be old and rare. Instantly Rick's trained eye picked out a perfect boxed set of space shuttle and launch booster with NASA decals and rocket-nozzle cowlings that marked it as an early issue limited edition. It would be worth over a hundred pounds without the box—double with it included.

Vaughn's eyes landed on a white display box, lined with red plush velvet and divided into thirteen compartments. In each compartment nestled a Mini, and there was not a scratch on any of them. Pride of place, sitting like a ruby in the central compartment, was a perfect Mini Cooper S. It had wide racing tyres, detailed interior (could Vaughn actually *see* dials and switches on the dashboard?), a white roof and bright blood-red bodywork. Vaughn felt his mouth go dry and his palms prickle with sweat as he guzzled the sight of that car.

Matthew focussed on the single model that made *his* heart pound. He had never seen one in the flesh and knew it only from catalogue pictures and dealers' descriptions. It was always labelled 'Most Rare':

A 113 mm customised Corvette Stingray supercharged, midnight black with glittering twinstars for headlights. It had a cutaway hood, and a vastly powerful, chunky looking engine that seemed to be all gleaming manifolds and exhaust outlets.

The paint amazed Matthew, yellow flares around the radiator grille blending to a dull red-hot-iron colour, then to blue with wips of faint white, like smoke along the doors and side panels—like smoke, or like the subtlest spray of starmist trailing down the autumn sky.

And the stallholder made it all seem possible, all real. . .

He was a youngish man with a plain, forgettable face and a smudge of brownish moustache. His hair was lank and straight, his expression rather vague. He did not seem to realise that a fortune was displayed around him, nor did he appear to care that every collector walked on without pausing to look, let alone to buy. His one concession to showmanship was a scuffed bowler hat perched oddly on his head, tilted forward to throw a shadow across his eyes. It was this ridiculous frippery that prompted Matthew to make his move.

"Haggle-box?" Vaughn wondered, still dazed with awe, as the boys walked forward slowly.

"I—don't know. Let's suss him first. Maybe it's all Taiwan fakery, right?" Matthew laughed uneasily, low in his throat. But they all knew he was wrong, that this stuff was real and the best they had ever seen.

"Lads. . ." the stallholder said, acknowledging their presence, the word drifting lazily by like a cloud over the sun.

"It's, um, some good stuff you've got here. . ." Matthew idly handled a white 1968 Volvo P 1800 de luxe that he knew was worth anything above seventy-five pounds. He used all his will power to force his mouth to sneer as he put the car down again.

"Interested?" The stallholder nodded towards the Volvo, uncharacteristically not bothering to readjust its position on the display table. Virtually every good dealer that the boys knew touched a valuable model every time it was picked up by a possible buyer, as though to reassure themselves that it was still there.

Matthew shook his head. "Naa. Not really my style. And, er, not rare enough. . ."

Rick struggled back a smile at his cheek.

"Now this," Matthew said, "is a different matter."

Tentatively he reached out for the Stingray, acutely aware that his hand was shaking. Incredibly, the dealer allowed him to take it, smiling slightly with his lips; silently, noncommittally, uncaringly. . .

Matthew did not notice the rest of existence fade away around him; his friends, the crowd, the hall, the street vanishing like smoke. The whole of reality and all meaning became concentrated in the car that rested solidly in his right hand.

Its workmanship was superb, unsurpassed, better even than the effusive descriptions of the model that Matthew had come across in the magazines. He could not bring himself to believe that the thing was die-cast, a pressing done on a machine. Someone surely had spent hours, hundreds of hours, working-in the minutiae that made the car all but unique. There was even a tiny speck of reflection from the driver's mirror and (Matthew actually gasped in admiration), microscopic markings on the speedo and rev-counter etched beautifully into the dash.

He could smell the oil of the engine, the soft leather of the upholstery. His imagination reached, reached beyond itself, and saw the interior of the cockpit around him and the night flowing by outside like a fast wild river of blue thunder.

His voice struggled up drily, just as if his mouth was crammed with feathers.

"What—uh—what do you want for it?"

Rick jabbed Matthew secretly with his elbow. This was not how they worked! Where was the plan, the opening gambit: Vaughn was not positioned right: there were not enough other people around to make the move unseen.

And besides that, the bad feeling in Rick's chest was stronger now, a warning pressure. Vaughn had already taken a precautionary step backwards.

"Matthew—" Rick began, but the stallholder's gaze swept like a slap across his face, frightening him to silence.

Now the dealer smiled fully and his expression changed. It was as though someone had lit a fire inside his skull. The dull eyes glowed with life, energy rose to the surface of his skin. His old bowler hat was menacing suddenly, not funny any more.

"The point is," he said, "you don't own a model like that. It owns you."

"I can pay. I work Saturdays. Look, I'll put a deposit down." The words tumbled out, falling loosely from his mouth. Matthew stuck a fist in his pocket and brought out what money he had, maybe ten pounds.

The dealer scratched his chin with a long fingernail.

"I can see you want it badly. And I don't blame you, there isn't another exactly like this anywhere."

"It's a legend," Matthew agreed.

"Of course, you'd expect to take the car away with you tonight?"

"Naturally."

"Well. . . You have an honest face, son. It's a deal."

The dealer beamed, white teeth and red lips, he looked flushed with health. Rick tried to grip Matthew's arm, but his friend had moved forward to take up the model again, handing over the money without noticing.

"Now, as a mark of good faith young man, would you sign this bill of sale—to prove we made an agreement?"

The dealer produced a square of paper and a black pen.

Matthew glanced at the bill and felt triumph roaring in his ears. There was no place to write his address, no proof of identity needed—only a dotted line for his name. He nodded, turning to Rick.

"Hold this, Dave, will you, just while I sign?"

"Matthew, but you don't know the price. The cost Matthew—the cost!"

Rick almost shouted, even though Matthew, in calling him by the wrong name, had given the signal to run. Vaughn was all but hopping nervously from foot to foot. The black Stingray felt like fire in Rick's hand.

Matthew leaned over the table, scribbled his name, gave the dealer a wink and then ran for it. In the first instant of his movement, the other two scattered also, sliding through the crowd that had suddenly solidified into something real, almost comforting. The heat and big, vague noise of the Assembly Rooms washed like the sea back over Rick and Vaughn as they ran, pushing and stumbling, for the exit. Rick glanced back once, but he had lost sight of both Matthew and the stall, the stall to beat all stalls into nothingness. Matthew bought it, he got that car, Rick kept thinking, he bought it, it's his.

Then the two of them were outside, gasping at the sharp cut of the air. They ducked sideways, around to the side of the building, then slowed and paused, leaning heavily against the wall, trawling for breath.

"H-hell, Rick, wh-what a game, eh?" Vaughn giggled out his fear and relief. The flat empty darkness of the college grounds stretched ahead, a huge easy hiding place.

"Hey, give us a look at that car. . ."

Rick brought the model closer to their faces, needing to squint because it was like holding a shadow up to their eyes.

"Wow," Vaughn whispered, "it's beautiful."

Rick marvelled, as Matthew had done, at the tiny perfections of the car; the seatstraps exact in every detail, the dashboard accuracies, the tiny plastic driver modelled right down to—

—There had been no driver! Rick had noticed that much when Matthew was bargaining. But now, behind the wheel, sat a minuscule figure wearing a stylish silvery jacket with smart red racing bands on the sleeve. The model driver's hair was red, his face. . .

Rick felt the scream rising, unable to stop it. Vaughn cried out and fell back against the wall.

Two diamond lights sparkled into brilliance.

Rick drew back his arm and launched the car far out into the night, losing sight of it. But before it hit the ground, there came a deep crackle of engine-life, a growl as power trembled through metal, and a flash of fire from the afterburners as the Stingray sped into blackness, far away and for ever.

The House that R'ork Built

"This it?" I wondered. Jeff nodded. His eyes were alight.

"It is the focal point, Louis. Can't you feel the lines of power converging here?"

I cocked a thumb at the pylons striding away over the fields and into the evening distance.

"Yeah, and hear them. . ." The wires were humming gently.

"Lines of power, you idiot, not power lines."

Jeff grinned. He was used to my sarcasm—never meant harmfully—and always forgave it. Well, I was the only person we both knew who'd tolerate Jeff's UFO mania. He'd been seeing aliens up every side alley since kindergarten, and writing about them, and joining clubs filled with other freaks and loners. Maybe it had started out as simple curiosity, a taste for the 'sense of wonder' he was always talking about. Maybe. But now it was his life, and I at least knew that he could never pull himself out of it. Jeff Collis had given up real life for ever and committed himself to his dreams.

"It's there, centred in that house. . ."

Jeff pointed through purple September gloom to the big square shadow of a house set alone in a half-circling of trees a hundred yards from the road. I thought it was where Glebe House had once stood, but that place was no more than a broken shell: this house was complete, lived in too. A single light shone from a downstairs window.

I looked up and down the road for Glebe, but there was

nothing; fields, a copse, the glitter of Raybrooke over a mile away, a nearby telephone box.

"Must be the wrong place. . ."

"What?"

"I said, they must have come from outer space."

"Who?"

"The family living in that big old house. Well, it's cheaper than the Holiday Inn."

Jeff chuckled, but emptily. I knew that his humour was being replaced by the mystic seriousness that usually infects him on a saucer-trek.

"Maybe they've parked their starship round back. . ."

"Come on," Jeff said, "let's investigate."

The truth was that I was nervous—not of a CE3K (Close Encounter of the Third Kind) you understand, but of making a total fool of myself in front of whoever we came across in our hunt for intergalactic beings. I had suffered my worst embarrassments in the company of Jeff Collis, and once almost had a backside full of buckshot when we were caught trespassing on private ground.

But none of that ever made any difference to Jeff. He had stars in his eyes and took no notice of trivialities like the law and mortal danger.

We crossed the road and leant on the gate that barred the long driveway up to the house.

"How do you know you're going to find something, Jeff?"

"It's nearly nine o'clock and it's Wednesday."

"Ah yes, that explains it all."

"It's in the BUFOD guide—the Bureau for UFO Detection, page eighty-two actually."

"Nine p.m. Wednesdays is when the aliens come out to play. . . ?"

"No Louis." Jeff's voice held a tone of carefully, and

barely, controlled patience. "Statistically, most UFOs are seen between nine in the evening and midnight. Also, Wednesday is the most popular day for sightings, and the twenty-fourth of the month is very significant in occult law."

"Occult?" I said. "I thought you were taking the scientific approach."

"Sure, but Man is a subtle mixture of the rational and the instinctive, just as the universe is a blending of the logical and unexplainable. I use my whole self in these investigations."

"Sorry I asked. But I'll tell you *something* mysterious. . ."

"Hm?" Jeff was busy making notes in his little UFO spotter's book. I pointed at the driveway.

"No-one's been along *here* all week, or maybe longer. No tyre marks in the soft mud, and the grass growing in the ruts is upright and undisturbed."

"Score one for you, Louis." Jeff smiled and clambered over the gate. What could I do but follow? "They probably arrived by matter transmitter," he said.

One thing that I constantly admire about Jeff is his determination, both to boldly go where no man has gone before, and to maintain his dignity while spouting the most ridiculous rubbish. You can never bait him: he'll never lose his temper or back down from holding his absurd beliefs. And he wasn't kidding with the matter transmitter idea.

"Maybe we could just do a very general interview with the people living here," I said. Jeff was two steps ahead, striding squelchily along the ridge between the ruts.

"I mean, say it's for our school magazine or something?"

"We'll take it as it comes. I've got the tape recorder ready, and the lump of iron."

"Oh?"

"It repels any creature of a vampiric or lycanthropic nature."

"Well thank God you remembered the lump of iron, Jeff."

93

"I knew you'd appreciate my foresight. . ."

He was deep into the mad-professor role now, so my function had to change from a vaguely interested and mildly sceptical disciple to a guardian and negotiator who would try to prevent these innocent country folk from calling the police and having him taken away. . .

We reached the gravel sweep in front of the house, but instead of knocking politely at the door, Jeff decided to 'scout round the back' for clues.

"For goodness' sake! Maybe they've got dogs—big ones, Jeff, with teeth. You know teeth—they chew legs off."

"Alien infiltrators would not risk detection by causing the disappearance of two local and well known boys. They would be more sophisticated—"

"Replace us with independently conscious holograms until their plan for world domination reached fruition."

Jeff stopped dead and swung around to face me, his expression one of deep suspicion, one almost of fear.

"Have you been reading my secret notebooks—because that's how *I* think they'll do it. . ."

He was serious! So I kept the smirk off my face and just shrugged.

"Great minds, Jeff, that's all. Or maybe we're telepathetic."

"Telepathic."

"I know what I mean."

"Well," Jeff said, "you're thinking along the right lines. You ought to join BUFOD, you know. We're always on the lookout for sharp new minds."

"Do I get a badge?"

"Anyway, if dogs were around they'd've sensed us by this time and set up a row." He paused significantly. "Come to think of it, I can't hear *any* animals."

That at least was a fact. Apart from the cool soughing of the wind in the dark pines, the world was silent: no dogs, cats, birds, traffic or poltergeists. Jeff made more notes in his book. I stared thoughtfully back the way we'd come.

"Actually Jeff, there is a kind of atmosphere here. I'm not usually sensitive to them, but I'll admit something's in the air—and it's not the smell of cows. . ."

I turned round for him to appreciate my wit, but he was already at the door, and it was open, and a warm rectangle of gold light cast Jeff in silhouette: lanky, stooped, with a haloed mop of curly, infrequently-cut hair. He was staring at the figure of a man who had silently appeared.

If I'd had any sense, I would have set off home at a run and not looked back.

I wandered over with a big stupid smile on my face.

"Look," I began to the man at the door, "I hope you don't mind. We're doing this research for our school magazine and—"

And I almost wet myself. Jeff was just staring in silence at the same thing.

The man was like a badly moulded lump of clay. That was my first snapshot impression. My second was a readjustment of the senses coupled with a feeling of guilt and shame that I should think so cruelly of someone disabled.

It was as though he could not stand upright, without the support of the wall. He was leaning weakly against it, his pale right hand pressed hard against what looked like bare pink plaster. His body was skeletal, the thin covering of flesh over the bones seeming white and bloodless. The man's hair was lifeless, greyish. His eyes were empty.

There was more than that. The house itself. Even as I thought it, a second inner voice told me severely that I was beginning to believe the same meaningless nonsense as Jeff. . .

But it was *there*, a vivid sense that the house was more alive than its occupant. The air was warm, rich with the smells of life—like a barn, but elusively different. And it was thickly heavy, greenhouse air, so dense that it very nearly shimmered.

"Perhaps," I said to Jeff, my voice quavering and quiet, "perhaps we should not disturb the gentleman. It is quite late, you know—on this *Wednesday*, the *twenty-fourth*. . ."

"No, he's just what we want."

I saw Jeff jab a finger to the side of the canvas bag that was slung over his shoulder; he'd set his tape recorder running, and the interview had started whether I liked it or not.

The man's mouth opened. Inside it was white and the pale tongue lay still like a dead fish on a bare sea bed.

"Pl-ease co-mein."

I wasn't sure if the man's accent was thickly foreign, or if the words themselves were so badly slurred as to be almost indecipherable. But what surprised me most was that the sound seemed to come from the walls and ceiling, a great blow of sound, a huge exaggeration of a man-sized voice.

Even Jeff took a step back, but as his silly impulsive legs walked him over the threshold, he turned his head and gave me a chuckling look.

"We've cracked it Louis. This is the *one*, man!"

"Something's cracked *you*, more like," I snapped, unnerved but not surprised when my impulsive legs carried me after him. . .

The house was rather bare, drab, unbearably stuffy—and odd. I felt the elusive strangeness of the place from the first moment. It scared me. The feeling reminded me of what a mouse might experience as it put a tentative paw on the wooden platform where the cheese lay. At any second I expected a monster to leap out in front of me or sneak up behind me. Thank God for Jeff's lump of iron—and this time I meant it.

We followed the man along a corridor towards a room off to the right. Another thing bothered me: he never took his

96

hand away from the wall. And, as the palm passed across, the plaster seemed to ripple like blancmange that had not quite set. Curious, I touched the wall myself, and the damn thing was warm! Underfloor heating I'd heard of, but this was ridiculous.

The man took us into the room and indicated some brownish armchairs opposite the door.

"Do—sit," he said, just about.

"Thanks." Jeff was visibly shaking with excitement, though I couldn't understand why. My shaking was of a different variety, because I was starting to have thoughts about kidnappers and psychopaths and. . . and vampires. The image kind of crawled out from under a wall of carefully cultivated disbelief and conventional education. Vampires didn't exist, so this weirdo couldn't be one. Q.E.D., right?

But I was still scared.

I sat in one armchair, Jeff in another. The material of the furniture seemed to be a sort of plastic that was slightly tacky to the touch; vaguely repellent. And for a few seconds it disorientated me, because I could have sworn the chair shifted the substance of itself to accommodate my exact shape.

Jeff started too. The man slowly lowered himself on to the sofa nearby, only releasing his contact with the wall when he was fully seated.

"Now then," Jeff began, notebook in hand. "Let's not beat around the bush. I have reason to suspect that you are not what you appear, Mr—"

"R'ork," came the reply, a frog's croak of a word.

"Mr R'ork. In fact, I strongly suspect that you are a being from another world, quite possibly from a planet beyond our galaxy."

Jeff beamed amiably, though his eyes were sharp and alert with anticipation. I could have curled up and died. However odd this R'ork person was, we must have seemed to be one egg short of a dozen, you know what I mean. . .

As it turned out, the situation did not develop as I expected. R'ork sat very still for perhaps a minute, then nodded gravely and returned Jeff's smile—that is, if the twisted travesty of an expression his lips made could be called a smile.

"You hum-ans are very sh-rewd. I th-ought my cam-ouf-lage was com-plete. . ."

"So you admit it!"

"I ad-mit it."

I couldn't believe what I was hearing! My alarm jumped up a number of notches as I realised that I was surrounded by loonies, me, the only sane individual for miles around. And I suddenly had doubts about myself—

The wall clock over the fireplace was melting.

"You must for-give me," R'ork continued shakily, "it is ha-ard for me to comm-unicate in th-is form. . ."

Jeff cast a triumphant glance my way: after years of humiliation and even persecution he was being proved right. All his dreams were coming true, and he smiled, even as R'ork began to disintegrate from something just about bearably human to something utterly and completely alien. . .

His body swiftly sank into the substance of the sofa, losing detail and colour, becoming plastic like a candle in an oven. The viscous movement of it was a little like a deflating balloon, a little like thick syrup overflowing from its jar. It was disgusting but, at the same time, fascinating. I sat transfixed for maybe two, three minutes while it happened, before I noticed something else:

The wall clock had become a blue globed eye: there was another one close by. And the fireplace had turned into a vast mouth that was beaming at us colossally.

"Aaahhh. . ." it said, a great outgusting like the storms of Mars. "That's better. I was having difficulty with that shape—such complexity packed into so small a size."

"It's what *I've* always said," Jeff piped up: you creep, I thought. "For all of humanity's failings, we are fairly advanced creatures."

"Some of us, Jeff," I spat out, trying to put anger, fear and a message of caution into the tone. Then I looked at that monstrous mouth. It could swallow us both without trying—and probably would, I guessed, despite its friendly expression.

"What are you? What do you want?"

I squirmed, realising that I sounded like a bad science fiction movie. The mouth and the eyes, however, considered my questions carefully before replying.

"I am R'ork of the Ischnoides race, from the planet Glareosus in the Vulpeculine cluster. I want to find out about Earth: I want to find out about—you."

"Why?" I wondered, indicating at the same time with my eyes to Jeff that he should try to make a run for it. If I could keep this great mouth-in-the-wall talking, and the huge alien eyes focused my way, Jeff could be in with a chance—as soon as he stopped scribbling stupid notes in his book!

"Like most species," R'ork said, "we of the Ischnoides have built up our population over the years to the point where we must seek new territories. Glareosus is now far too small and cramped, and our urge to expand and explore has driven us outwards to all parts of the galaxy. I came here—and fortunately so, as I did not expect such pleasant and inquisitive company!"

R'ork's red lips parted in a smile. Its teeth were white, and sharp, and as big as housebricks.

"So. . . Your intention is to use Earth for your own purposes, to make it a colony."

"Indeed. Intelligence *and* curiosity! I am well favoured."

I was running out of questions by now—and nerve. Jeff just sat there nodding eagerly like a bookworm at a philosophy lecture, so I reasoned it was down to me to act.

I reckoned that a mouth embedded in plaster could not inflict much damage if I stayed well away from it, so my plan was to make a dive straight for the door—not going near Jeff, who would have to take his chances. They would not be great, I thought, if he continued talking to this alien as though it was a next-door neighbour.

I tensed up ready to move. And the chair clenched around me.

It happened in an instant. In the space of a breath the arms of the chair rippled, suddenly bulging and pulsing with veins: artificial fibre became skin, foam filling became muscles. R'ork's huge impassive eyes swung to glare at me, and the mouth in the wall began to laugh.

That's when I stopped thinking and started acting. I had a metal ballpoint pen in my pocket, and did not hesitate: I held it hard in my fist and jabbed it down into the chair.

R'ork's bellowing laugh lifted upward to a scream of pain. The chair-arm bled, and the whole piece of furniture began thrashing around me. Jeff, who had been watching all of this with mouth open, put up his hands as though to stop traffic.

"Louis. . . No—this isn't the way. We must compromise with these creatures. Reason with them. . ."

"Stuff your compromise!" I yelled. "I'm being eaten by an armchair, and you want to *reason* with it! Just get yourself moving!"

The muscular feel of the thing around me abated, became jellylike and amorphous. I pushed myself away from it and ran.

I leaped headfirst through the doorway as the door began to swing shut. While it did, it was transforming into a lobe of flesh that reached itself towards me.

"Jeff! Get out!"

Jeff of course stood there like a nail, torn between saving himself and establishing détente with an alien blob from the Vulpeculine cluster. He and I glanced up together as the ceiling sagged and became a searching tongue.

I cried out in terror, and left my friend behind.

R'ork had not stopped his screaming during this, but now it was more like a roar; angry, predatory.

A bubble swelled in the wall beside me. It expanded to a face—a white and featureless thing, just enough of a face to be able to see and speak to me.

"Face facts," R'ork said, a gentle voice punctuating the barrage of sound that the house was making. "You cannot win, because you cannot predict my actions. What do you know of me? What will I do next?"

"You bloody murderer. You killed Jeff!"

"How do you know that?" R'ork began, but I was already swinging my fist.

The face opened into a tunnel lined with teeth, and I just managed to divert my blow as the tunnel clamped closed with an adder's hiss.

Now I was almost out of the place, which was beginning to drop the façade of being a house: Banisters became bones, plaster lost its smoothness and sharp edges, windows membraned over and grew opaque.

"Come on," said the letter box, "let's sit and talk about this."

A chair surged into being from the soft toffee of the floor. It was a gesture of a chair, more like a cupped hand held out.

I jumped round it, pulled aside the floppy front door and belted down the driveway.

The cold air of evening made me gasp more than my mad dash for the road. Once I looked back as I sat astride the barred gate.

The house that was R'ork—illuminated internally some-how—towered and sang around the ruined shell of what must have been Glebe House, probably the template for R'ork's first camouflage on this Earth.

It led me to wonder if maybe the creature could not move easily, in which case it would still be there when the police arrived: police, army, marines, any damn body I could get out here!

I hurried to the telephone kiosk, keeping a wary eye open for R'ork or any of its manifestations. I had no money, but an emergency call would be free.

I picked up the receiver. No dialling tone. R'ork's voice.

"Hello Louis. I told you that you couldn't win. Meet my son."

In my hand the telephone writhed into something red and grinning. The glass of the booth thickened over. And suddenly I couldn't find the door.

Highscore

Benjamin Peterson is one of those kids I just don't like. He's pleasant enough, never says anything against me, but maybe that's it: maybe he's simply too *nice*, you know? He has soft good looks—lots of fair curly hair and clean blue eyes, an attractive smile. Mr Sellars our Games' teacher calls Ben Peterson 'pretty boy'. But then, Sellars himself looks like King Kong's ugly sister. . .

Ben gets a bit of ribbing from the other kids at school too, sometimes, and smiles his way out of it. He's found his secret weapon in life, what my mum refers to as a winning smile. She reckons he'll grow up to make Prime Minister, though I think he hasn't got it in him. Ben's not mean enough.

I first met him to talk to at the town Gemini Centre, which is a kind of youth club that was set up to keep us vandals off the streets. It works too, so I won't be all that sarcastic about the place. Loads of kids go there—all kinds of kids, even ones who were actually vandals and will be again once they lose interest in Gemini. Most turn up for the sports; there's tennis and badminton, long alley skittles, a bit of grass for field games, and stuff like darts, pool, you name it.

The reason *I* trek down the centre most nights of the week is to play the space invader machines. I think it was a local businessman who put up the cash to have three or four of them installed. He laid out the first year's rental too, but that was paid off inside two months with the amount of money that got stuffed into the coin boxes. And I'd bet he makes a fat profit from us poor adolescents as well. Still, as I said, it keeps us off the streets.

My favourite game is 'Alien Attack', because it's fast and bright, and because the stereo sounds of battle match the high quality of the computer graphics. And it's a table top game also, which I find more comfortable than standing to play for hours. And I *mean* for hours, since a one-pound-for-six-plays outlay will give me a whole evening's games, once I start highscoring and picking up free bonus games. One time last spring, Mr Briggs who runs the centre had to switch off the power at the wall to get me to leave. I started to argue, so he grabbed me by the shirt collar and hauled me out. I was a little bit annoyed. . .

Next night, when I was thinking about doing some damage, old Briggs pushes a fifty-pence into my hand and tells me to keep out of trouble. And I did. He's OK, is Briggs.

Another feature of 'Attack', one that's common actually, is that you can select from one-player or two-player mode. Usually I go for solo fighting, since just about every kid I know simply isn't up to my standard. That's not boasting, it's just a fact. Sometimes I try a partner though, like about a month ago when I asked Sonya Demaris if she wanted to play with me at the table. The bruise hung around on my face for a fortnight. . .

I wasn't really in the mood for partnering this night when Benjamin Peterson wandered up and asked if I fancied a battle. I couldn't figure his reasoning because at least one other of the machines was free, and I wasn't the sort of person Ben would want to make friends with.

Still, a game is a game I always say. I nodded at the empty soft-seat opposite.

"Six-play?" I asked, knowing that within a half-dozen games I could have blitzed Peterson and accumulated enough points to earn the first of a run of bonuses. Sly, eh?

Ben tossed a pound coin on the dark glass of the table.

"I'll pay," he offered. And who was I to argue?

I slotted the coin into the side of the machine, selected the right mode and pressed for start.

"You go first," I told him, "and watch out for the red meanies."

The machine came to life. First, an upward spiralling whirl of rainbow stars broke from the darkness, accompanied by a fanfare of spacey music and a taster of the battle-sounds that would build up through the game. Then, red and gold curtains shimmered into being, dissolving slowly to reveal the prologue that I now knew by heart:

ON THOUSANDS OF WORLDS AMONG THE MILLIONS
OF STARS SCATTERED THROUGH THE ENDLESS
UNIVERSE, THE ETERNAL BATTLE OF RIGHT AGAINST
WRONG, OF LIGHT AGAINST DARK, OF GOOD AGAINST
EVIL IS BEING WAGED AND WON. . .

The drumbeat background synth started up: dub-dub-dub-dub. . . This would continue to the end, growing faster as the advancing lines of alien spacecraft moved down the screen.

Ben saw the first of them—an unimportant green vanguard—and began zapping.

"They're only worth a point each," I told him, "and they won't fire back. Ignore them."

Ben carried on firing, and that's when it occurred to me that this kid had no clue about the tactics of space-gaming. He didn't even realise that his ammo count was dwindling and could only be replenished with enemy craft destroyed. Well, I wasn't going to tell him everything, was I?

Within three minutes Ben's defensive shields had been lasered into fragments, and he'd sustained damage to three of his four singularity engines, plus some dangerous bulkhead weakening on the bridge.

The end came quickly. Gorgeous blue sparks were already spitting from the dorsal section of the ship, and Ben was having difficulty swinging it around to repel the swarm of enemy star-saucers massing for the kill.

Then the red supercruiser of the alien leader dropped into view and erupted green fire from all its forward guns. The thing hissed like a dragon: the synth-beat was a fast, regular dubba-dubba-dubba-dubba sound—

One energy bolt touched the heart of Ben's ship and the whole games machine rumbled. The ship burst into a globe of spinning splinters and silky mists of light. There was a funny little music-box funeral march and the end message:

PLAYER ONE GAME OVER SCORE 772 CADET RATING. . .
PLAYER TWO PREPARE. . .

"Not bad Peterson," I said, "for a cadet. Now watch the starship captain."

Right from the first instant of the game, I felt I was a part of the machine: my thumb welded perfectly into the concave warmth of the start-stud, my fingers found the starship joystick and firing button as though by themselves, my eyes seemed to see everything that was happening on the screen without needing to look at details. I *knew* what to do almost before the machine generated the situation in glittering pixels.

I forgot all about Peterson, who must have been bored out of his brain just sitting there watching me clean up. Wave after wave of alien craft rushed down at me, trying to draw me out towards the centre of the screen, where they could surround me and finish me off. No way! I wiped out dozens of green outriders, blue cruisers, violet destroyers—taking my time, but acting within the rhythms of the game, moving into feigned vulnerability when *I* chose to.

It worked—it always does, because the machine is only a machine. . . I had plenty of laser bolts left, plus two photon torpedoes; these I always kept to the end, both of them. One was no good by itself.

Now the game was hot and humming, every light possible glowing. Space was filled with the sizzling static of energy screens and the cosmic spitting of lasers. I swept the ship round, mopping up stragglers—but not too many—luring out the red supercruiser. When it appeared, I loosed off the first torp—which it dodged—but the second was already flying to the point the supercruiser reached at the end of its manoeuvre.

There came two nearly simultaneous sunbursts, the first non-scoring, the second taking out the supercruiser to win me an extra 1,000 points and the game.

The screen began its concluding fanfare—curtains of light, triumphant synth melodies and so on. But I was already grinning, readying up to key-in my highscore.

The space scenario cleared, and against a backdrop of slowly falling star-rain the previous records came on. . .

Mine was not at the top, like it should have been. I always sign myself 'Kirk', it's my gaming name, and the scoreboard read like this:

BRAG	—	23,468	RATING CAPTAIN	2nd CLASS
KIRK	—	23,220	RATING CAPTAIN	2nd CLASS
ANNA	—	22,946	RATING CAPTAIN	3rd CLASS
PETE	—	21,447	RATING STARPILOT	

And so on down the ranks to the cadets. Tonight I'd scored 23,136, which gave me second and third positions on the machine—but not first and second as I'd expected.

My stupid I'm-the-best smirk vanished.

"Who the hell is this Brag kid?" I wondered out loud, then remembered Peterson's existence. He was looking at me like he already knew.

"I've never even seen him in here," I went on, angry and puzzled, "but he must have been playing today, since I was top of the scorers last night. . ."

Peterson started walking away. I jumped up and snatched for him, leaving my clutch of free games open for the gannets to take.

"Hang on." I caught up to him by the door and grabbed his jacket. Briggs, who was serving colas at the hatch, noticed me and gave me one of his glares; no trouble from you, Adrian, OK? it said, without him even opening his mouth.

"Tell me about Brag. Who is he?"

Peterson twisted himself away and went outside. I followed. It was nine o'clock and getting dark, the sky all purple with smouldering clouds. I could smell autumntime in the air.

"He's like a kid," Peterson said, kind of mumbling it. I took that to mean Brag was childish.

"Does he go to the High?"

"No, he. . . he just bothers me, Adrian."

"What do you mean? Bullies you?"

"Not bullies. He just won't leave me alone. . ."

Peterson hung his head and I thought pretty boy was going to cry. Ordinarily I'd've left him to sort out his own difficulties, but that left the question of Brag's highscore and my pride. There was no way someone who signed himself like that was going to beat *me* at Alien Attack—Adrian 'Captain Kirk' Rossington, the town's true best.

"Know where he lives?" I asked Peterson, whose face changed at the words, "or where I can get hold of him?"

"He'll turn up with me tomorrow. At seven."

"Sure?"

"I'm sure."

I watched him walk away down the road, fading and brightening as he reached and passed under the streetlamps. And right at the end of Morgan Avenue, before he turned off, he looked back, and I could have sworn he was smiling.

Next day. I arrived at the Gemini Centre early, straight after my tea at five-thirty. Briggs was just opening up and stared at me suspiciously when he saw me hanging around at the front as he unlocked the doors.

"What's going on, Adrian—no homework tonight?"

"Did it all last night, Mr Briggs," I lied, slick as oil. He grinned and we understood each other without needing to say more. I jingled my pocketful of coins.

"It's games' time. I got some aliens to smash."

"Well," he said, flipping on the lights, "that's what life's all about."

Too true, I thought: the only other choice was nine-to-five or unemployment. At least this way I sailed among the stars.

I didn't waste time buying Coke or chocolate bars, but got straight down to a few practise runs on the machine. Because of the unusual circumstances; no juke box playing or kids laughing around me, the game didn't run as smooth as I wanted. On my three-life first run I lost two lives within the 5,000-point mark and struggled on with my last man to notch a score of 16,857. This was poor by my standard, damn poor when I thought about what Brag had achieved—invisibly by all accounts—the day before. Games two and three warmed up for me, and my second pound play saw me over the 20,000 point line each time.

A few regulars drifted in between six- and seven-thirty, by which time I had only a pound left, and was thinking about touching Briggs for a can or two on the slate.

I wondered if Brag had chickened out, or if Peterson had maybe decided not to tell him about what had become, in my mind, an important challenge. But just as I was beginning to feel both relieved and frustrated, the door swung open and the two of them walked in. . .

Peterson looked scared, I could tell that right away. There he was, hair all highlighted and slicked back, wearing the latest fashion gear, but pale as a corpse and with an expression as miserable as December.

This other kid, this Brag, was weird. He was short, almost deformed, in his baggy, sacklike trousers and jacket. His hair was dark and straight, no style to it at all, and he looked, well, evil is the word that first came into my head. Brag looked evil, scared of nothing: more than just out for some fun, you know?

Peterson brought him over to me, but didn't want to look into my eyes. He stared at the ground, like someone who is ashamed of a sinful act.

"This is Brag." He almost whispered it. Brag said nothing, but glared like he wanted to rip my throat out. I put on my meanest expression, but my stomach turned over.

"Let's play," I said. No way was I intending to find out anything about this boy, other than how good he was on the machine. I felt like I remembered feeling once when I came across the body of a cat that had been run down by a car. I could only have been seven or eight. It was a summer day and the heat had given me a headache. I pushed over the cat with my shoe: the animal had seemed quite normal, but very still. Underneath it was crawling, and I turned aside just in time to bring up my lunch at the sight.

Now I swallowed down hard and tried to hide my grimace—and I did my best to forget all the questions that came clamouring into my head: like, who was Brag and where did he come from? And why was Peterson mixed up with him at all if Brag was such hassle?

I sat down, sliding into my usual place with my back to the window across the room. This meant that I did not have the distraction of stray daylight, nor of people passing; something that could happen at a critical second and mean the difference between success or failure.

Brag took his seat. The kid's eyes were not empty or vague, as his appearance and silence might suggest: but they were filled with nothing that I could name. They were like eyes that had never learned the human emotions. Animal's eyes.

I thought then that I was being really stupid and that this was likely Brag's gambit, to spook me into a nervy and average game.

I dug into my jeans for playing-money (sacrosanct no matter *how* thirsty I was for Coke), but Peterson already had it in his hands and threw down three pound coins which burred and rattled on the tabletop glass.

"Best of eighteen games, that's three sets of six—"

"I got some idea of maths, Peterson," I grumbled, but tipped him a wink at the same time and tried a smile. His face stayed as cold and grey as a dead fire.

"After you Brag," I offered, being polite—but really to study the form of the kid as he played.

He didn't nod or acknowledge me, and I had the feeling that he would've taken first shot regardless of what *I* wanted.

The machine came to life. What had been a dark plate of glass, sticky and smeared with fingermarks, dropped into a depthless view of deep space peppered with star crystals. Lights whirled up as though stirred by a spoon, and the prologue shone out:

ON THOUSANDS OF WORLDS AMONG THE MILLIONS
OF STARS SCATTERED THROUGH THE ENDLESS
UNIVERSE, THE ETERNAL BATTLE OF RIGHT AGAINST
WRONG, OF LIGHT AGAINST DARK. . .

Brag opened his mouth and laughed, a dry and woolly sound like his throat was packed with dirt. The kid's teeth were yellow, some were black, his tongue looked white and bloodless.

I felt myself shiver, even though only yards away kids were rocking to a new chart sound or giving Briggs some stick about the price of his drinks. I could feel the company of other people behind me, but I was looking at something that might have been lying six months in a churchyard.

After the fanfare, the go-bleep sounded and the game began. A black slick of hair fell over Brag's eyes as he bent his head forward, and he hunched down so that I couldn't see anything of his expression.

He began to fire, systematically mowing down opposition as the vanguard ships eased into view.

After a couple of minutes he had not dropped a point, and I had mapped out his play. He was one of those kids who—by having spent hours working out the pattern of the whole game—operate like machines themselves. It takes memory, a certain amount of dedication, no imagination at all and involves no risk. It is, ultimately, the most boring way to win, and the most effective.

Brag stayed on for twenty minutes, won three straight games and rubbed me out.

I tell you, I felt humiliated and angry. It wouldn't have been so bad if I had *enjoyed* watching his play, but that had no entertainment value at all: it was tedious and predictable. I wondered why, this being the case, Brag had not topped the 25,000 line to win a Captain 1st Class accolade. I mentioned it to Peterson, who shifted his eyes jumpily as though Brag was about to pull out a stick and belt him a good one with it.

"He could do it," Peterson whispered, "but you wouldn't have been tempted by the challenge. He made it close so that you'd fall into the trap by playing him."

"What trap?" I asked. There was no money involved, and if the kid only wanted to satisfy his pride, well let him!

Peterson nearly answered, until Brag's hand crept across his like a great spider, curling its legs over Peterson's fingers. I knew Brag's hand was cold. I don't know how, but *that* fact I would have gambled on.

Peterson shut his mouth with a click.

Courtesy-of-play dictated that I should begin the second set of games, though I knew damn well that Brag wouldn't bother with etiquette. I slid the second coin off the side of the table, slotted it and pushed for start before anyone could complain. And Brag didn't, he just lifted his big, ugly squarish head and glared. . . I was looking at a dog about to bite me.

I played carefully, knocking out smalltime enemy ships without endangering myself, not going for the big stuff and not enjoying myself either. It wasn't just that I knew Brag's dark, burnt-out eyes were on me: I felt a physical pressure in my chest, a horrible squeezing around my heart that seemed to get worse as my score notched up.

Ten minutes in I lost my third life and was almost doubling over with the pain. Sweat was appearing on my forehead and trickling down into my eyes. I looked at Peterson and gave him a sickly, abashed grin. He didn't seem too hot either, his skin pale and doughy. And he was scared witless.

I think it was in that second what had been a cloud of doubts and suspicions became the solid fear that I was into something dangerous. Brag wasn't simply a kid who was obsessed by winning a table game. He was someone else; maybe some*thing* else—a creature from another planet, or from a deep, dark corner of our own world. I didn't know for sure. What I *did* know was that Peterson had got himself tangled up with Brag and now, probably too frightened to do anything else, was setting me up as well.

It would work, too, unless I did something about it. My score was currently 3,000 behind Brag's, but regardless of individual game-totals, we were defining win-or-lose according to the final tally after eighteen games, when Peterson's three coins had been used.

Brag began his mechanical playing on game five, took that and two more, by which time I was nearly 7,000 down and looking for inspiration.

But at least—in a strange way I couldn't understand—Brag's concentration on the game had caused the pain in my chest to lessen. I had time and inclination to look around, and it occurred to me gradually that Brag kept his head low and close to the glass for a reason. . .

We paused after game fifteen, having played for two hours. Outside, the sky had darkened almost to black: around us, lights were low so that kids could dance in the right atmosphere and play the machines undistracted. The only spots shone on the two dartboards across the room.

I wiped perspiration off my face and went into my big act.

"It's hot work," I said, "losing to this genius. I tell you Brag, I've never seen anyone play like you. I reckon you've got this challenge taped up. . ."

His lips stretched a grin, but did not part. I had the vision of a chameleon's lizard mouth, an instant before its great sticky tongue leaps out to trap the dragonfly.

"How about a Coke? Hey Ben, lend us some cash will you, I'm a bit short tonight."

Peterson didn't argue. I reckon he was beyond everything except dread. He passed over a couple of pounds. I stood up stiffly and went across to Briggs, had a word with him and then stuffed some of the change into the jukebox. There were still a couple of quiet, smoochy tracks to run out before my selection came on.

We had three games to play. Brag was on 24,370, I trailed

with 18,089 and had much ground to make up. But it was possible, if I played well and if Brag played badly.

He opened with game sixteen, and was thirty seconds into it when the first rock song burst out of the juke. I saw his thick greyish fingers falter and he lost a life.

"Turn it up!" I called, and the shout was echoed by some of the others on the dance floor. Briggs pushed up the volume and hooked in the disco lights as I'd requested.

The effect on Brag was startling. He just couldn't do anything right. The drumbeat and splintering guitars, the flickers of light skittering on the table glass ruined his game completely. He finished on 24,986, still 2nd class rating. And it was my turn.

What Brag hated, I loved. I bobbed my head and tapped my feet to the hard, fast rock tracks and dropped into the fantasy of being a starship captain. Nor was I cautious now. I took all the risks I could, feinting the ship this way and that, zipping and zigzagging through space after the big game. The machine hummed hot and ran smooth. I mopped up points with no trouble.

It was the final game, I was on my last life with a score of 24,133, and space was thick with aliens; weird spiders hurrying along a webwork of laser light. On the jukebox, my selection was coming to an end. The dancefloor was emptying now, kids giving up, and no doubt Briggs was losing his patience, wanting quiet too.

I went into my usual endplay, beaming-out a few fighters, doing damage to a bigger destroyer. . . My score edged up to 24,685. Brag could still win this, and he was leaning over watching every move, his face eager with anticipation.

Then the alien Supercruiser hove into view amidst whirlpool light. I dodged a crossflash of lasers, swung to firing position and stab-stabbed the torpedo button. The first missed and flared, the second hit bang on target, ending the game and jumping my score over the 25,000 mark. I slumped back, drained, and happier than I've ever been.

I keyed-in my highscore and seconds later it came up:

KIRK	—	25,685	RATING CAPTAIN	1st CLASS
BRAG	—	24,986	RATING CAPTAIN	2nd CLASS

He didn't wait to see more. With a snarl he pushed himself away and ran to the door, banging into kids, blundering his way through, vanishing into darkness.

I went after him with Peterson, who was shaking, but we didn't venture outside. Not for any good reason, you understand. . .

Then I felt my one and only moment of sympathy for Brag, which evaporated as soon as it came.

"He must come from somewhere terribly dark," I said quietly to Peterson, "and somewhere terribly cold. . ."

And he probably got drenched walking back there too, because there was one hell of a thunderstorm over Grimsborough Hill ten minutes after Brag left.

Burning

They told me that I would never leave here, and I believe them, for I have tested that truth.

At first, when I was very young and they brought me to Genco, I thought it was a school. There were lots of other children here, and we played and we learned. My parents were upset to let me go, but they had been instructed to do it by the Dominus, and were honoured to obey even though their hearts were broken. They said that they would come to see me as often as they could, but Deevis who leads us said that would not be possible. They wondered why, I remember: and I wondered why. But now I know.

I remember, too, my first talk with Deevis. In those days, in the early time, he was gentle and kind, but still there was a little fear in his eyes. We walked away from the Complex into the grounds where the birds sang and the trees whispered. We sat in an open space that was bright and warm with sunlight, and Deevis gave me some chocolate.

"Brin," he said, "I want to answer some of your questions. That is necessary if you are to enjoy a happy life here at Genco."

He paused for a moment and looked at the sky, as though reflecting. Then he looked at me with eyes that held hope and curiosity and many other things. He smiled.

"You are a very special boy, you know. In the same way, all of the children who come to us are special. The Dominus knows of your existence. He calls you The Favoured Ones."

"Bless and keep the Dominus," I said, without really thinking: it was what I was meant to say.

"Bless and keep him," Deevis echoed, and smiled in a way that I could not quite understand.

"You know Brin, of course, that you are studying with us and not at a normal school because you are not like most other children. . ."

I nodded. He went on softly:

"Here you will be trained both to control and to use your powers in the service of the Dominus. Tell me, what do you understand your powers to be?"

I thought about that hard, because I had never put it into words before. What I did had always been a feeling. I said, "I can make the trees shed their leaves. I can make people grow old. I can make the sun and moon spin like coins in the sky. . ."

It made me chuckle, because that was funny to see. But Deevis stared at me with clouds passing in his eyes.

"That is an interesting way to put it, Brin. And indeed, that is how you see it happening. Scientifically, we say that you have the power to pass through time—STT, Spontaneous Temporal Translocation. When people grow older, it is because you have jumped into their futures, years ahead to them, but an instant in time to you. Do you understand?"

"Yes sir," I answered, but I was not sure that I did.

"Good. But there is one other piece of information that you must also understand and remember. Otherwise, life for you and for us at Genco could be very dangerous. . ."

Deevis tried to smile in a friendly way, but I saw the corners of his mouth twitching, just a fraction.

"Strictly speaking it is not true to say that you pass through time, Brin: rather, time passes through you. You are like a lens that focuses the energy we call minutes and seconds. Now, what happens if you focus sunlight on paper?"

"It burns," I said. That was easy. "The paper burns away to nothing."

"Yes, that's right. It burns. Listen to me now—although we may want you to move into the future—to make the trees shed their leaves—you must *never* open yourself to it completely. You must never jump as far as you can, because the whole energy of your life would be focused into the millionth part of an instant. Do you understand me, Brin?"

This time I could not nod. Deevis said:

"Never ever make the moon spin too fast, Brin. Yes?"

I can't remember now if I answered him, because it interested me so much to see him trembling.

Over the years I learned many lessons and saw many strange sights. At Genco the techniks taught me to use my power sparingly, so that I thought of seconds like grains of gold that were not to be squandered. Once, when I was late back to my room after talking to Karel, my truest friend, I jumped-on to morning so that the doors would be unlocked. Deevis was there waiting with two men from Security. They were frightened, all of them, but Deevis was angry too. It was the first and only time he ever hit me for what I had done. Both of us knew then that he would never dare to try it again.

I told Karel about it later and she sympathised. I think, out of all the people I knew, she was the kindest, and she alone did not look on me with fear.

Her gift, she told me, was to see into people. Not really into their bodies, but in a thought-feel way into their heads and their hearts. I suppose she saw something of what would become of them.

"And what will become of me, Karel?" I wondered. The day was bright and scented: outside the Genco Complex I think people called it May.

Karel stared at the sky. "There will be many days like this, Brin. But dark days too. Days of war, I think. . ."

"Like what—days like what?"

"With me beside you, loving you Brin."

Karel leaned close and kissed me. Her blonde hair crossed my eyes and made the sun shimmer. I lay with her and I thought, as it was happening, that Burning must be like this. This is how it would be to make the sun twirl like a coin.

Some time later Deevis talked to us about the War. He spoke to all of us together, as well as seeing each of us alone. As his voice boomed in the auditorium I watched the faces of the others: some of them did not look quite like people, but each of their expressions was the same.

"So," Deevis said in finishing, "we must all play a part in helping the Dominus to fight the threat of the Merican-Sovyet advance. Our future lies in saving the futures of everyone. God bless and keep the Dominus."

"Bless and keep him," I whispered with the rest, and wondered where Merican-Sovyet might be in the world. . .

In the months that followed, many of the Genco children left to fight in the War. They were really young men and young women, although in what they said—and in the way that pride and terror were mixed in their eyes—they still seemed so young to me. One of them, a geopath called Sonda, said he was part of a Genetically Controlled Counter-Terrorist Force. Deevis had told him, Sonda said. But when I asked what the words meant, Sonda didn't know and we both laughed about it. He waved back at me from the front gate, and that was the last I saw of him.

Winter came and life grew dull. I wanted so much to jump on to the warmer days of summer, but I realised that it would mean leaving Karel behind: that is, the Karel-of-this-moment. If I did it, she would be six months older and I would not have aged at all. I knew too, that if I started to ignore my lessons and drift futurewards out of curiosity or selfishness, then I would not be able to stop. Compulsion to *see* how the world went would draw me on through eternity. And, as Deevis had warned, that could be dangerous: to look upon forever would mean the Burning.

But I was bored. I saw Deevis about it.

"I don't understand," I told him, "why you don't send *me* to the War. Am I not fit and strong like—like Sonda for instance?"

"You are fit and strong, Brin," Deevis said, "and the Dominus would be pleased with your loyalty. As for Sonda, he was useful as a weapon to be dispatched and, if necessary, sacrificed. But you—you are too valuable to be sent away."

"Why?" I wondered. Deevis considered his answer carefully.

"Because the world has never seen a power like yours. We are not sure exactly what it is, or what it might develop into. Only future generations of temperopaths will solve that puzzle."

"Future generations?" That confused me, because my parents were not Favoured, and I had no brothers or sisters who might want—

Then Deevis told me about Karel and our child, and that although this was our purpose in the eyes of the Dominus, Karel truly loved me and wanted our baby to live and he brought up at Genco.

I asked if I might see Karel: she had not been allowed out of her rooms for weeks, but Deevis shook his head.

"She is resting, Brin, and under the care of many doctors. . ."

I held Deevis's arm gently.

"I am going to see her, Deevis," I said, only quietly, and he did not stand in my way.

Karel looked beautiful in her bed, despite the automedic machines that glinted and moved around her. Her eyes lit as she saw me, but then grew dark and moist. She began to cry.

"You know," she said, "that they have done this to us? The whole reason for us being here was to produce what is inside me?"

I nodded, yet only realising it as she spoke.

"I don't think," Karel went on, "that they are really interested in me—maybe in you Brin, because of your gift. They want our child! They want to see what she is and what she can do. They are going to use her, Brin, to help win their filthy War!"

Karel's hands were shaking in anger. Red monitor lights came up on a wallscreen.

"'She'," I whispered. "You can see that?"

"I only feel it," Karel said. "I see that the future glows with light." Tears dropped from her eyes, and she covered them with her quivering hands. "The future is so bright, Brin. So bright. . ."

I think I had never felt so sick and betrayed as I did then. I felt hot rage building up in my chest. It came to me that for all these years I had believed the word of the Dominus (bless and keep him, a mind-voice sang), but that perhaps he was wrong, and that the Merican-Sovyet was fighting for what was right. And good.

I sat beside Karel on the bed and held her. Alarms chattered nearby and shrieked in the corridors. The arms of the machines quickly withdrew.

"We can stop what we fear," I said gently, not frightened now, because she was with me. "Our daughter does not have to be a weapon for the Dominus, or an experiment for Deevis to watch. We do not have to be prisoners here any longer. . ."

I sounded strong, but I knew I could do it only if Karel was with me.

I heard footsteps hammering closer, and men were shouting.